"I may not ...
to take a bat ... *Savanna* ...

"Do you have any idea how cold that water is?" Rasch asked.

"I've been cold and wet before," she answered, giving him a long, heated look. "Why don't you build up the fire while I'm gone?"

She undressed near the stream and took a deep breath, then plunged into the icy water. She washed quickly, then just as she was sure she was half frozen, she heard a splash behind her, and felt herself caught in the judge's arms.

"You're going to catch pneumonia and turn into an icicle," he said in a voice hoarse with emotion as he tightened his arms around her.

"Would that be so bad?"

"I'd probably come back and sit in this stream until I was as frozen as you," he said. "Then we could melt together." He lifted her in his arms and carried her to the fire. "Stand here," he said, and began drying her with his towel.

By the time they were dry, they were warmed by the touch of hands and kisses that heated the blood and fired the nerve endings with anticipation. When he laid her on the sleeping bag, she didn't need it to be zipped to protect her from the cold. The mountains had become a rain forest, and their inner fire a volcano ready to erupt.

"Unbraid your hair," Rasch whispered. "I like you free and wild. . . ."

WHAT ARE *LOVESWEPT* ROMANCES?

They are stories of true romance and touching emotion. We believe those two very important ingredients are constants in our highly sensual and very believable stories in the *LOVESWEPT* line. Our goal is to give you, the reader, stories of consistently high quality that may sometimes make you laugh, sometimes make you cry, but are always fresh and creative and contain many delightful surprises within their pages.

Most romance fans read an enormous number of books. Those they truly love, they keep. Others may be traded with friends and soon forgotten. We hope that each *LOVESWEPT* romance will be a treasure—a "keeper." We will always try to publish

LOVE STORIES YOU'LL NEVER FORGET
BY AUTHORS YOU'LL ALWAYS REMEMBER

The Editors

Loveswept 512

Sandra Chastain
The Judge
and the Gypsy

BANTAM BOOKS
NEW YORK · TORONTO · LONDON · SYDNEY · AUCKLAND

THE JUDGE AND THE GYPSY

A Bantam Book / December 1991

ISBN 0-553-44134-5

Published simultaneously in the United States and Canada

Bantam Books are published by Bantam Books, a division
of Bantam Doubleday Dell Publishing Group, Inc. Its trademark, consisting of the words "Bantam Books" and the
portrayal of a rooster, is Registered in U.S. Patent and
Trademark Office and in other countries. Marca Registrada.
Bantam Books, 666 Fifth Avenue, New York, New York 10103.

PRINTED IN THE UNITED STATES OF AMERICA

OPM 0 9 8 7 6 5 4 3 2 1

For Nita, who's very special.
Thanks for making me feel that way too.

The Judge
and the Gypsy

Prologue

"What am I going to do, Zeena? My father intends to kill Judge Webber, the man he holds responsible for my brother's death." Savannah Ramey ran a slender hand through her luxuriant ebony tresses.

"I know, my child. It's the way of the Gypsy; An eye for an eye and a tooth for a tooth."

Savannah sighed. She'd come to Zeena's tent for answers, though she knew there were none. Skeptics doubted the circus fortune-teller's clairvoyant powers, but Savannah believed in the old woman. Still, there were times when answers didn't come, and others when their meaning was obscure.

Savannah's delicately arched brows knit together in a frown. "I'm afraid, Zeena. My father is too old to settle a debt. I've already lost Tifton—I won't lose

Father too. There must be something I can do. Please, will you help me?"

"I cannot, my child. This time you must look beyond the anger and grief to the power inside you."

Savannah's jet eyes glittered with emotion. "All I want to do is make the judge hurt the way we hurt. Death is too easy. I want *him* to lose part of his heart and live with the loss."

"Part of his heart?" Zeena echoed.

Savannah nodded. "The problem is that Judge Webber's only interest is the law. He lives alone. He has no family, no lover, no one to lose."

The old woman reached across the table and took Savannah's hand. She'd loved this girl close to eighteen years, since she was a bright nine-year-old grieving the death of her mother. She'd watched Savannah learn to walk the wires, trying desperately to replace the woman who'd been the heart of their little circus world. Zeena had seen Savannah help raise her daredevil younger brother, Tifton, blinding herself to his faults, loving him unconditionally. Now Savannah could feel the current of Zeena's emotional support flow from the older woman's fingertips to her own, and prepared to listen carefully to the fortune-teller's advice.

"Remember this," Zeena said softly. "A man without love is most in need of it, and suffers the most when it is lost."

Savannah considered the fortune-teller's words. And then suddenly she understood. Revenge was up to her. With the ways of a Gypsy, she could capture his heart. Then she could break it. She stood and jutted out her chin.

"I understand now what I must do. I'll give him what he needs most. Then I'll take it away."

"What will you give him, Savannah?"

"I'll give him myself."

One

The first time he saw her, she was nude.

It was October, and Rasch Webber was sitting beside the French doors in his study, reading the latest *Law Review*, when he felt a strange burning sensation on his shoulder. Turning, he saw her.

She was standing on his patio, four stories off the ground. A late night fog swirled about her, masking her features, except for a glorious mane of silver-colored hair that fell across her shoulders and draped her body in a shimmer of reflected light.

He decided that he'd fallen asleep and was having an erotic dream. As he stared, the chrome clock in the foyer struck midnight. He glanced at his watch as if to confirm the exact time of her appearance: twelve o'clock. Rasch rubbed his eyes. He was definitely awake. His gaze went back to the patio; he was certain the vision would have vanished.

She was still there, legs long and slim, arms slightly extended as if to say Here I am, come and get me—if you dare. She wasn't smiling exactly. In the distance her expression was one of mystery . . . or sadness. He couldn't see her eyes, but her arms fell slowly to her sides in what Rasch could only interpret as a gesture of censure.

A sharp gust of air swept the cloud cover from the night sky behind her, and her head tipped back as though she were responding to a voice no one else could hear. For one brief second she stood bathed in moonlight, her silver hair glistening like gossamer sprinkled with beads of stardust.

Rasch caught his breath and remained absolutely still. If this was a dream, he wanted it to continue. If it wasn't, he knew instinctively that his slightest movement would send her skittering off into the night.

"Are you real?" a voice whispered, and he realized that it was his own.

But she didn't answer.

Abruptly a curtain of fog seemed to envelop her. There was a faint tinkle of bells, and she was gone.

For a long moment Rasch sat in stunned disbelief. Then he sprang to his feet and dashed through the open doors. But there was no one there, only a lingering low-hanging cloud. Air heavy with mist covered the patio like a gauzy tent. An elusive fragrance wafted momentarily and disappeared. The lone sound was that of the rustling leaves.

Though the night air was cool, Rasch felt as if his body were burning. His heart was pounding, and his breath was quick and fast. He felt alternately cold and hot, calm and excited.

Rasch turned back inside, reaching for his phone to call his doctor. Then he stopped. What would he say? *This is Judge Horatio Webber, and there was a beautiful spirit on my patio. No, I don't know how she got there, or where she went. But she was there, I saw her. Now she's gone. Am I losing my mind?*

Rasch dropped his hand.

Hell, what he had to do first was convince himself. Either she was there, or he was seeing ghosts. And Rasch didn't believe in ghosts. She had to have been a dream. There was no way a woman could have been on his balcony—even if his body was still singing in response to her electrifying presence.

Judge Webber had never had a waking dream, but he'd read somewhere that stress could do strange things to a man. He might be known as Georgia's Super Judge in the courtroom, but even a tough guy could have an erotic vision if he was *too* tired and *too* lonely. And tonight, he conceded as he stretched his shoulders and went back inside, he was both.

Too many evil people. Too many questions without answers. Too much indifference. Too much isolation for too many years. For some time he'd felt as if he were struggling against a wind that was stronger than he, as if no matter how much he moved, he remained in the same place. He was still reeling from the results of his get-tough DUI policy.

The boy had come before him, brash, charming, contrite, mitigating his guilt in a traffic accident. He'd lost his license and he didn't know the car was stolen; the man he was riding with said it was borrowed. It was the woman who'd run the red light, not him.

But Tifton Ramey was drunk when arrested. And Rasch had made an example of him and sentenced him to jail. Then, unexpectedly, in some kind of freak happening, there'd been a fight with another inmate, and the boy was dead.

Rasch's firm stand on driving under the influence, his policy of getting drunk drivers off the road to protect the public, had resulted in a nightmare. A boy who didn't deserve the death penalty was dead. Rasch knew that if he had fined Tifton Ramey and put him on probation, the boy would still be alive. But his death had been a fluke, unforeseen in his sentencing.

The story made the front page of the newspapers. It still haunted the judge, who was supposed to be hard as nails, and he couldn't even talk about it. No wonder he was seeing spirits on his balcony. He needed to get away and do some serious thinking about his future.

Once he'd made up his mind that he'd imagined the vision, Rasch took a cold shower and forcibly put the incident behind him. It wasn't real. Rasch Webber was a man who dealt with reality, and reality was the harsh truth of the boy's death. He had to confront that, and his own responsibility in the matter, and stop manufacturing visions in the night as an escape.

God, he was tired.

If she was a dream, she was a recurring one.

The next time Rasch saw his woman of the mists was at Underground Atlanta at a street cocktail party for the politicians, and the rich and famous, of the city of Atlanta. The street was choking with smoke left over from the fireworks display moments earlier. As instructed by Jake Dalton, his old friend and self-appointed campaign manager, Rasch had been greeting the movers and shakers who shaped the political structure of Georgia's state government.

Just as the fireworks display ended, Rasch felt the beginning of an uneasy burning sensation concentrated at the back of his neck. He caught himself rubbing the spot absently, so frequently that Jake asked him if he had a headache.

"Yes," Rasch answered, knowing that it wasn't a headache so much as an odd feeling of anxiety, an awareness that tingled his nerve endings.

"I'll find an aspirin," Jake said, and disappeared into the crush of people.

Rasch made his way across the cobbled street and stood in the darkened doorway beneath the wicked-looking gargoyles and intricate carvings along the eaves. He leaned back in the shadows and let the swirl of noise drift across him. This was the part of running for office that he hated, the fund-raising. All he wanted to do was talk to the man on the street— not these men, many of whom who cared more about their own futures than their state's.

But money guaranteed a platform from which he could plead his case for reforms within the court system. Money would give reality to his vision—if he decided that justice could better be served by his taking political office than by his remaining on the bench.

He felt a sudden electric jab at the nape of his neck like a finger of fire, and lifted his eyes in the direction from which the beam of energy seemed to emanate. He'd felt that sensation before.

In the haze-filled air he saw her.

The woman from his patio was standing beneath one of the great globes of light like a mystical goddess from some fantasy. It was her, his midnight vision. *He recognized her*—not only visually, but because of a disturbing physical heat she created in him that he couldn't explain. She was the same woman, yet this time she looked different. Her hair was auburn and woven with brightly colored ribbons that ended in streamers that seemed to cover her body in satin rainbows.

Her face was again shrouded in shadows, but even across the crowd he could sense her sorrow. There was a slight sheen on her face as if of tears, and she shook her head, making a motion toward him that, as on her first appearance, bespoke condemnation.

A fragile, wary look about her touched him physically. He felt a pounding of energy rush through him; the feeling was almost sexual and yet, at the same time, he felt an unusual hint of fear. Who was she?

Rasch looked around. Nobody else seemed to notice her.

"All right, my lady of mystery," Rasch said, and started toward her. "If you aren't a figment of my imagination, it's time we met." Quickly he threaded his way through the noisy patrons and tipsy party guests until he reached the lamp. She was gone.

"Damn!"

Rasch climbed up on the base of the lamp post and surveyed the throng. The woman was like smoke. One minute she was there, piercing his peace of mind with her gaze. The next she had vanished like a wisp of fog. He swore again.

"Rasch? What are you doing?" Jake had found him. He was bearing a small glass and a concerned expression. "I don't think that the judge climbing a flagpole is the kind of image we want to portray for the next governor. Maybe you'd better not have anything else to drink."

Rasch ignored Jake's remarks. "Did you see her, Jake?"

"Who?"

"The woman with the ribbons in her hair. She was standing right here."

"No. I've seen women with glitter, diamonds, lace, and a couple wearing hats, but no ribbons. Why?"

"I've got to find her. She's driving me crazy."

Rasch could tell from Jake's expression that his friend was having serious doubts about his sobriety.

"Sorry, Rasch old buddy, I don't think I can help you find a woman who isn't there, but here are your aspirin. Come down from the pole. You're just tired."

Rasch came down and swallowed the small white tablets. If his oldest friend already thought he was hallucinating, then telling him that the woman had appeared once before, on a balcony four floors up, would certainly be a mistake. Not even Jake would back a candidate who fantasized about mystery women.

"Tonight," Jake was saying, "we've tried to plant the idea in everyone's mind that you're a future candidate for political office. That's all we want right now. Let's shake a few more hands."

"You're right, Jake. I am tired. Since we're both going to that conference in Asheville on law and order, I think that I'll drive up to Amicalola Falls next week and spend a few days hiking the Appalachian Trail. You can pick me up at Bly Gap, and we'll drive into Asheville together.

"Want some company on the trail?"

"No. After fifteen straight months without a break, I'm ready for some peace and quiet."

"Maybe a few days in the wilderness is just what you need. Find yourself a lady friend to take along. Let yourself go, Rasch. Stop being so much in control."

Rasch nodded absently and moved away from the waiter hovering nearby with a tray of empty glasses.

The burning sensation at the base of his neck was less potent but still there. He glanced around. The woman was still there too. He couldn't see her, but he could feel her. At least he thought he could. Maybe he *was* hallucinating.

The scent. He recognized it—that same scent from the balcony. He knew who'd worn the perfume, even if she was no longer visible. He rubbed his eyes. Damn, he didn't believe in ghosts.

And then he saw it.

At the base of the lamp a single red satin ribbon curled across the pillar of white concrete like a smear of blood.

For the rest of the week she was in his mind constantly, frustratingly. The connection was so strong that over and over he turned his head, expecting to catch a glimpse of her in his courtroom, or in the hallway as he moved about the building. The fragrance that was uniquely hers filled his nostrils, and the burning sensation at the base of his skull stayed with him, but he never caught sight of her.

On Thursday afternoon the jury returned a guilty verdict in the case he was hearing, and Rasch scheduled sentencing for the following morning. By midafternoon on Friday he was in his 4x4 and headed north. In less than an hour the hazy gray shape of the

Blue Ridge Mountains appeared in the distance. With every mile he covered, he felt the tension inside him lift. He'd spend the night under the stars.

Rasch took in a deep breath of fresh air and rubbed the back of his neck. The worrisome tingling seemed to have disappeared. If only he could erase the vision of the woman from his mind—and more important from his body, which kept responding to the thought of her lying beneath him. . . .

"Are you sure this is the route he is taking?" Savannah Ramey sat in Niko's battered truck in a patch of woods and wondered why she had ever thought this would work.

"I'm sure. Between Cheno and me, the judge hasn't made a move that we don't know about. The màn is a robot. He gets up at the same time every morning, wears the gray suit every Monday, the pinstripe every Tuesday, eats at the same restaurant, parks in the same place—"

"Okay, I get the idea, Judge Horatio Webber is a creature of habit." He was also entirely too appealing. His stunned look of disbelief when she'd first seen him on his balcony had almost made her change her mind. If he'd been anyone else, she'd have been attracted to the disturbingly handsome man who was her sworn enemy.

"Exactly. Tough, honest, but he's still a sucker for somebody in distress."

"That's what I'm counting on. If he decides to check the truck, it won't crank, will it?"

"No," her circus companion replied, his concern over her scheme still plain in his expression.

"I don't want him to realize that this is a setup. It's better if I keep him confused."

"If he isn't confused by a woman who appears on his balcony as a blonde, in a crowded street as a redhead, and on a mountain as a dark-haired witch, I don't know what else you can do."

Sometimes *she* was a little confused. How could a man regarded as a champion of the underdog be the callous killer of her brother?

"Exactly," Savannah said with grim determination. "I don't want him to know what is real and what is not."

Her plan had to work. Niko had grudgingly helped her so far, but once the judge appeared, she was on her own. She had only ten days to carry out her plan—ten days to make Judge Horatio Webber fall in love with her.

Savannah got out of Niko's truck and unwound the mass of raven-black hair she'd kept in a braid. She let it fall across the shoulders of her white peasant blouse while she shook out her bright print skirt and ruffled petticoat. Next she placed her grandmother's gold chains around her neck, added her mother's Gypsy earrings, and Zeena's ankle bracelet with the silver bells that jingled when she walked. The first time they met face-to-face, she wanted to meet Judge Horatio Webber as a Gypsy.

"I'll go back to the motel and wait for your call," Niko said with obvious reluctance. "You have the number?"

"I have it. Don't worry."

"I still don't like it, Savannah, but since you insist on going through with this . . . look—there he is.

Won't you change your mind while you still can? You could be the one to get hurt."

"No, Niko. I have to do this." Savannah gave the old man a quick kiss, moved onto the roadway, and started walking up the mountain. She was banking on the judge's reputation as a man of honor and responsibility. He wouldn't drive away and leave a woman on the side of the road.

She shivered, not from the cool air but from anticipation. She'd carefully worked out each sequential step in her plan, but there was always a chance that the judge wouldn't cooperate. Then she heard the sound of his jeep.

Taking a deep breath, Savannah stopped at the side of the road. Just as the four-wheel-drive reached the stretch of road behind her, she stepped from the gray shadows into the path of the jeep and stuck up her thumb.

"What the . . . ?" Rasch hit the brakes and slid sideways to a stop.

He blinked. It was very early. Wisps of fog rose from the pavement, curling into transparent little patches that reflected the parking lights on his vehicle. He closed his eyes and opened them again, slowly. This was no dream, no hallucination. There was a woman in the road.

No, the apparition in the road wasn't just *a* woman, it was *the* woman, the silver-haired woman from the balcony, the auburn-haired woman from the street, the woman who'd plagued him unmercifully for the last week. He still had no clear picture of her face, but he knew it was she. And more than that, every nerve ending in his body recognized and responded to her presence, just as they had before.

This time she was wearing a long print skirt and no shoes. And her hair, her glorious hair, was neither silver nor gold; it was as black as a midnight sky, and wildly tousled as if she'd just rolled from a man's bed.

He swore in the silence.

"Please?" she said in a low, melodious voice. "I seem to be stranded. Could you give me a ride?"

Her words became an almost verbal caress, and he felt his body surge in response.

He'd seen a truck with the hood open back in the trees. Was she alone? Was this some trick to lure him into a trap? He couldn't see anyone else.

"I'm alone," she said, almost as if she could read his mind. "I sent Niko down the mountain to get help. He'll come back for the truck. But I don't have time to wait."

"Why? What are you doing up here?"

"I'm meeting someone. Please, may I get in? It's cold in the woods," she said simply, as if that answered his question.

It didn't. But for now he'd go along with her story. Hallucination? Spirit? He might be tired and confused, but this woman was real, and it was time he got to the bottom of the mystery. "Get in."

He heard the fleeting tinkle of bells, and suddenly she was inside the small truck, filling it with her distinctive, elusive fragrance, and the curious feeling of excitement that had seemed to follow him for the last three weeks. She was here, the object of his uncertainty and desire, and he was determined to know what kind of game she was playing with his emotions.

"That fragrance," he asked, "what is it?"

"It's made from the blossoms of the tea olive tree. Do you like it?"

"It's very unusual."

"Yes." She didn't volunteer any more, but placed her knapsack between her knees and settled back as if she were someone he'd known a long time, someone with whom he was comfortable enough not to need to make conversation.

"Where are you going?" he asked, slowly letting off the brake and listening to the crunch of the loose gravel on the road as the tires found traction and began to move.

"To Amicalola Falls. I plan to do some hiking. You?"

Once he decided to go along with her request, he'd stopped being surprised. "That's where I'm going too."

"I'm glad. It's very early," she said. "I've come a long way. I think I'll take a nap."

"But wait, who are you? What's your name?" he started to ask. Except before he got the second word out, her eyes were closed and she seemed to be asleep.

Rasch shook his head in disbelief. Where had she come from? She had a backpack, but her feet were bare and scratched. How could his mystery woman possibly be in the same place as he, at the same time? From the moment she'd appeared on his balcony, his power of reasoning seemed to have deserted him.

Certainly she hadn't been far from his thoughts either asleep or awake. He'd constantly looked for her, worried over his recollection of what he'd seen or imagined. He'd begun to doubt his own recall after a time. Now, here she was, sitting beside him, almost as if he'd conjured her up.

He looked across at her once more. The lines of her face were clear now. Her pale skin was like that of an Old Master's Madonna. Lips as red as the dahlia that his mother grew in a bucket at his back door were closed serenely in sleep. Long velvety lashes feathered cheekbones that more nearly belonged on a painting than a real person.

She was an enigma, this woman of silence and grace, yet beneath that calm was a hidden fire. He couldn't see it so much as he could feel the tension. The interior of the truck felt charged with a strange energy, and he shivered.

Whatever she was, and wherever she came from, she'd appeared to him three times, and he had to know why. There were answers to his questions, and he meant to have them. He'd take her to meet her friend, for it suited his purpose to know more about her. He gave the vehicle gas and moved up the mountain.

Savannah Ramey let out a silent sigh of relief. She'd passed the first hurdle. She hadn't expected it to be so hard, lying to him. From a distance the square cut of his jaw hadn't been so intimidating. She hadn't seen the laugh lines at the corner of his eyes, or their steely gray color that seemed to pin her down. But it was more than the way he looked, it was the sensual power of the man, more potent at close range, that had forced her to retreat into silent confusion.

She liked men, but after one mistake as a teenager, she'd never had a serious romantic relationship. She was never in one place long enough to develop intimacy anyway, so her circle of friends had been limited to the circus people, and she was the boss's daughter. Being apart from the mainstream had suited her fine, but it hadn't suited Tifton.

Tifton. She forced her attention away from the man beside her and back to her plan. According to the information Niko had gathered by following the judge and eavesdropping on his conversations with his friend Jake, she should have four or five days to reach the halfway point on the trail. Five days later the judge would meet Jake Dalton, who would drive him on into Asheville. She had ten days to complete her plan, and she had no intention of failing. She owed that much to Tifton, to the laughing, happy boy who'd died because of this man—this vigilante judge.

Rasch was content to study her as she napped or pretended to, until he was certain that she wasn't up to something else under cover of sleep. By that time they were well into the foothills of the mountains. "Do you plan to sleep all the way?"

Savannah opened her eyes and gave him a half-amused, half-sultry look. "Maybe."

"That's easier than talking."

"Yes. Thank you for the ride."

Her voice was vaguely musical. There was a breathlessness, a baffling hesitation in the way she paced her breathing between words, almost as if she were rehearsing lines she'd never read before.

"I probably should have taken you back to town. But it's time I learn why you're haunting me."

"Haunting you?" She hadn't expected the direct approach. She laughed uneasily, her confidence wavering. "Am I?"

The sound of her laughter seemed to ripple across the silence. "Yes, dammit. Since I first saw you on the patio, you've been driving me crazy."

"I don't know what you're talking about." She forced her gaze away from his strong face to his hands, which gripped the steering wheel with an unsettling intensity, and wondered for a fleeting second what they would feel like caressing her flesh. What was happening to her? She couldn't back down now. She'd learned enough about the judge to know that he couldn't accept not knowing. That would be the key to her reaching him. "Until now," she said as evenly as she could, "we've never met."

He didn't believe that for a minute. But he could see that direct confrontation wasn't going to work. "Technically you're correct."

He smiled, but the smile didn't reach his eyes. "We have never met. I'll accept that, for now. Let me ask you another question—where did you come from?"

She knew that his gaze saw through her, probed her inner recesses and aroused unwonted and disconcerting feelings within her, and she protected herself by looking away. "It doesn't matter," she said. "It only matters where we go from here, doesn't it?"

She'd been prepared for disbelief, questions, accusations. But the curious, calm acceptance by the man beside her was unexpected, and therefore intriguing. Who was becoming bemused?

Judge Webber wasn't especially tall, but he gave the illusion of height and strength. He hadn't shaved that morning, and there was a shadow of stubble across his chin that enhanced his virility. His dark blond hair was neatly cut, but his tendency to run his fingers through it kept it permanently tousled.

His masculinity filled the cab and threatened to engulf Savannah.

In his courtroom, where she'd disguised herself so that she could watch from a back seat, his piercing gray eyes were often hidden behind thin black-rimmed glasses. Today they were unveiled, and she could feel the brunt of their disturbing penetration.

There were other differences today as well. From a distance she hadn't noticed the strong beat of his pulse, exposed by the open button on his shirt, the way an unruly lock of hair fell across his cheek, the tightening of the muscles in his upper arms when he turned the wheel. From a distance she hadn't noticed his disquieting maleness. Perhaps this wouldn't be as easy as she'd thought.

From the first she'd liked his voice. There was a resonance there, a boldness that said he was willing to enter a debate and give it his best shot. But he didn't rattle easily, and he wasn't going to make it simple for her to defeat his innate logic. She'd forced him to take her along, and he'd agreed. Now it would be a cat-and-mouse game until one of them became the victor. Fine, she'd accept the challenge. She would win.

"Perhaps you're right, mystery lady. Perhaps it isn't the destination but the journey that's important."

Everything about this woman challenged him. She was a puzzle to be solved, and he was more than game. For the first time in months he felt fully alive, body, mind, and soul. "Do you consider yourself a philosopher?"

"No," she said, "I don't think so. Though I believe that we each have a function in life. I suppose you could call me a voyager."

"A voyager? A traveler, an adventurer—in search of?"

"Knowledge, I suppose. Truth. And what are you?"

"*Knowledge? Truth?* Rasch felt a tingle of unease. She'd given back the answer he might have spoken. "If I had to put a name on my life's mission, I'd have to say that I'm a crusader."

She turned her dark eyes on him, fusing her gaze with his to the point that he lifted his foot from the gas for fear of running off the road. "So we both travel the same path."

"Perhaps. A crusader and a voyager, each with a quest."

"Ah, then you are searching too." Her voice was almost a whisper, though it was clear and passionate. "What are you seeking?"

"What all crusaders seek, I suppose—wisdom, justice. I try to make things better, to right certain wrongs."

"And are you always right, Judge Webber?"

"How do you know my name?"

She broke the connection by raising her gaze to the sheaf of papers stuck behind the visor.

He followed her movement and read the name on the envelope that threatened to slide from its niche. *The Honorable Horatio Webber*, superior court judge, it said, and gave his office address.

So she wasn't psychic and she wasn't a mind reader. Her powers were strong, the vibration of his nerve endings attested to that, but she relied on normal answers just as any other mortal would.

Mortal? Why had he even thought that? He was getting squirrely. What he needed was coffee and food. Surely this creature of his imagination ate human food. He was going to have a hard time finding pomegranates and figs in the mountains of north Georgia.

"Shall we have breakfast together? There's a little place up the road where fishermen and hunters stop for a good meal. Nothing fancy, but it's filling."

"Fine," she said, and rewarded Rasch with a smile so warm that it brushed away the last of the gray fog in his mind. She was a woman, and he was a man. Perhaps that was enough.

So maybe there were no figs and pomegranates in the North Georgia Mountains. Maybe she'd settle for coffee and doughnuts. Not food for the gods, but they were hot and sweet, and hot and sweet seemed just about right.

Two

The Gold Rush Grocery and Café was tucked into a hollowed-out place in the side of the mountain. There were three parking spaces and room for one camper. This morning most of the regulars had already come and gone, so Rasch had no trouble stopping in front.

He climbed out and started around the jeep to open the door for his hitchhiker. He took her pack and threw it into the back, then stopped. She knew who he was, but he still didn't have a name to call her. The passenger door opened wider, and a bare foot extended itself and slipped to the ground with a tinkling sound. He'd heard that sound before. Then he saw it, an ankle bracelet with little silver bells. She'd been so still in the jeep that the bells hadn't made a sound.

"Is something wrong?"

Her voice sounded like the bells, which sounded like her laughter. Every movement, every sound, was a kind of music, and he smiled again without being aware that he was doing so.

"Your feet," he said. "You aren't wearing shoes."

"No."

She closed the door and came to stand beside him. "Is that important?"

"No, I mean yes. You can't hike a mountain trail without proper boots. You do have boots in your backpack?"

Now it was her turn to smile. "No."

He shook his head disapprovingly. "Some preparations you've made! No matter—they carry hiking and camping supplies inside. You'd better buy a pair of boots."

"All right, and tell me what else I'll need," she said. "The only thing in my pack is my sleeping bag and some food."

"Don't you know that it can get cool on the trail at night? The weather forecast is fair for the next couple of days, but in this area that can change within hours."

"Oh, dear. I guess I ought to confess that I've never camped out before." *On a trail,* she ought to have added. Circus performers spent a lifetime camping out. But she had her own van, with her own bed and supplies. This was different. "Please help me, Crusader."

"I suppose I'd better, or I'll end up rescuing you again." He laughed, and Savannah found his warm laughter surprisingly sexy. She'd heard of bedroom eyes, but never of bedroom laughter. Yet suddenly she had an all-too-delicious sensation of sharing a cozy bedcover with Judge Horatio Webber. "I'll make you a deal," he went on. "My help in exchange for some revelations of the truth about you. Agreed?"

"Revelations about me? All right. There are many truths, Horatio Webber. I'll reveal mine, but only when the time is right."

Savannah followed him inside. He didn't know it yet, but the die was cast. She would share his journey in exchange for the truth—only she knew that there were no friends to meet her, and that the quest she was embarking on was to claim his soul.

Rasch felt a tinge of excitement. She'd agreed to tell him what he wanted to know. He wished he felt more confident about the wording of her promise.

Inside the little store, Rasch picked up white cotton socks, and brown wool ones, then helped Savannah select a pair of boots that felt to her as if she had lead weights on her feet.

Savannah exchanged the brown socks for red.

Rasch selected a pair of jeans, a T-shirt, and a heavy flannel shirt to go along with the boots. He gathered up packets of food and canned goods and added them to their cache. As the grocer rang up the goods, Rasch shook his head. The truth had already cost him $98.00, even before breakfast, and he had yet to hear a word of it. But to find this woman he would have paid a lot more.

Savannah wandered into the restaurant side of the building while he paid their bill and carried their purchases to the truck. He found his sultry traveling companion at a corner table between two windows. She didn't acknowledge his presence; instead, she stared intently out of the window.

"What are you looking at?" Rasch asked, sliding into a chair across the table from her.

"There's a chipmunk out there, beneath that rotten limb by the fence."

Rasch looked at the spot she'd described. He couldn't see anything except brush and trash. "Where?"

"Be very still, and he'll come," she said, reaching across the table, laying her hand across his. At her touch came the same jolt of awareness that he'd felt in the street. It danced across them like an arc from an electrical connection. She looked startled for a moment, then slid her hand away, but in the void left behind there was a shivery feeling almost as concrete as the sound of the bells.

"Look now," she whispered, touching him again. Her palm felt rough, as if she'd been cutting wood or using a hammer.

At that moment the little brown animal scurried out, stopped, and looked up at the window as if he'd been called. After a long, still moment, he turned and darted away.

Savannah turned her gaze to Rasch. She didn't speak, but somehow he knew that just as she'd communicated with the chipmunk, she was communicating with something inside him. Yet even as he felt a response well up inside him, Rasch suddenly rebelled. He didn't like the idea that this woman was trying to control him, even in this small way. With a growl he jerked his hand away and broke the visual contact between them.

"Where's the coffee? I'm hungry!"

Without turning her head, she answered, "It's coming."

It was. The waitress appeared from behind a swinging door, bearing two thick mugs, and filled them with steaming strong coffee. She laid out napkins, butter, jelly, and a pitcher of cream.

"Your food will be here terectly," she said in the curious mountain dialect. She studied Rasch and Savannah for a moment before she turned away. "You know you're supposed to be wearing shoes in here, lady."

Savannah looked startled. "No, I didn't know, I'm sorry. I have boots in the car. Shall I get them?"

"No," the woman said, "just keep your feet under the table so nobody will know. You don't look like hunters."

"We're camping," Rasch explained, then wondered why he did. Campers didn't wear Gypsy skirts and ankle bracelets with bells over bare feet.

"Well, take it easy. If you ain't used to wearing shoes, them boots are gonna do a job on your feet."

Rasch had already considered that possibility and determined that after he got some answers to his questions, he'd persuade Savannah to turn back. It wasn't that she didn't belong in the mountains; everything about her said that she did. But his plan to be alone and do some serious thinking would be compromised by her presence.

Savannah didn't comment. She wasn't worried. Years of circus performing had callused her hands and her feet to the point that she doubted anything would hurt them.

The morning sunlight had burned off all the night mists, and the day was gloriously golden. The trees were speckled with orange and yellow and red patches where the leaves were taking on their fall colors. Fall was late this year, but now winter would come swiftly to the mountains.

Rasch hoped that the sleeping bag his companion claimed to have brought would keep her warm. Mountain air was deceptive, especially in late October. The weather report said that conditions for the next two days would be bright and clear. After that the picture became hazier. The possibility of a cold front moving in always brought the chance of unexpected rain and sometimes snow.

The waitress was back. She laid out thick white plates piled with scrambled eggs and crisp bacon.

Rasch picked up his fork and speared a section of bacon. "All this cholesterol isn't good for the body," he said. "I usually have bran flakes and juice."

"That's sensible, but the body sometimes has needs that aren't sensible, don't you think?"

There it was again, that burning sensation. Except this time it concentrated itself in a spot just below his left ear. The current seemed to dart down the nerve endings to his fingertips, and he could hardly grip the fork.

"Who *are* you?" he whispered huskily.

She dropped her voice and answered, "I am called Savannah."

Not that her name was Savannah, but that she was *called* Savannah. "Why?"

"Because that is the city where I was born, in a special place in a glen of sweet grass and gentle night creatures. And you are called Horatio, which means keeper of the hours, strong, steady. Is that what your mother intended for her son, why she called you Horatio?"

"I doubt that time had anything to do with it. My mother thought that Horatio was an important-sounding name."

"Your mother wanted fame for you?"

"I don't know. She just liked the sound, I think."

Savannah raised her coffee cup and took a sip. "I like sounds. I like to hear, and touch. People don't listen anymore. And when they do, they don't hear."

"Do you always speak in riddles?"

"No. Do you always ask questions?"

"Yes, I think I do. I think that it's important for a person to ask, and know, don't you? How else do you find the truth?"

"Ah, but what is truth? One person's truth is another's fantasy. I prefer answers from the heart, not the head."

"As a child you must have driven your father crazy. He probably never knew when you were telling the truth or when you were pretending."

"When I was a little girl, my father was a man of imagination, too, but even then there were times when he told me to be patient. That much I did learn. All things come to the one who waits."

Rasch smiled. He was finding it difficult to picture this beautiful, baffling woman as a child, and he knew that she'd been no more patient in childhood than she was now. If she wanted something, she'd get it. He was having a hard time deciding what she wanted from him. Maybe he ought to put pretense aside and simply ask.

He did. "I know that you're the woman from my balcony, the woman from the street, and I suspect that you planned this meeting as well. Didn't you?"

His gaze was direct, penetrating: It made her heart beat faster. "Perhaps. Perhaps not."

"What do you really want from me, Savannah,

whose flashing black eyes telegraph such mysterious messages?"

"I want to know you, that's all." She really wasn't a woman of mystery, but she intended to make the judge believe in the fantasy.

"Know me? I can't think that you came to me on my balcony and again at a party because you wanted to get to know me. Why didn't you just ring my doorbell?"

"Would you have let me in?"

Yes, he could have said, because I wanted, no, needed, to know that you were real—not some imagined spirit that I'd conjured up.

What he said was "I suppose not."

"You're being very honest, Crusader, and you deserve the truth from me. What do I want from you? Are you sure you want to know?"

"I'm sure."

"Then the truth, Crusader"—she tilted her head and gave him a burning gaze—"comes with a price."

"And the price?"

"That you take me with you."

"Take you with me?" He couldn't conceal the shock in his voice. He couldn't conceal the curious little quiver in his gut either. "Why would I want to do that?"

"Because I'm here. Because I wish you to. Because you and I are . . . connected."

"What are you, some kind of witch?" Rasch drew back, a frown of disbelief on his face. "I warn you, Savannah, whoever you are, I don't believe in superstition."

"Don't worry, Judge Webber," she said quietly. "I'm not a witch. You're not a man who believes in spirits.

You're a man who believes in facts and reality. Well, I'm real. And that's what makes you uncomfortable, isn't it?"

"Yes," he agreed, "I think it does. I don't like what I can't explain. And for the moment I can't explain you."

"That's all right. I understand, truly I do. And I'll try not to sound mysterious, or make you uneasy. I'll admit that I seem to have some kind of telepathic connection with animals. They don't talk to me. But we, I don't know how to explain it, except to say we connect, just as you and I do."

"I can believe that." Rasch drained the last of his coffee and forced himself to think of ordinary things as he swallowed the last bit of eggs. Savannah was right. Bacon and eggs were a luxury that he ought to indulge in more often. He'd forgotten how satisfying a real old-fashioned breakfast could be. He'd forgotten how nice it was to share breakfast with a woman. He knew that he was not only considering her request, but accepting it.

He wasn't quite sure how or why he was sitting there, calmly having breakfast with a woman who communicated with animals. In some secret part of his mind he'd known all along that this was no chance meeting, that she had some well-thought-out plan by which she arranged to meet him, and she'd captured his interest in a way he could neither justify nor explain.

And that intrigued him. For now, so long as he understood that this obsession was mutual, he was willing to play along until he could learn the truth. She obviously had a plan, and he wanted to know what it was.

After all, he reasoned, she was only a woman, though she was the most beautiful woman he'd ever seen. He was mature in mind and body, and he could handle whatever she was planning. *More rationalization,* an inner voice chided him.

"I understand that there are certain people who have the rare ability to communicate with animals," he admitted, "and sometimes telepathically with people too."

"Yes. But I don't—" Her voice faltered, and she lowered her eyes. She was giving away too much, too much that even she didn't understand. For a moment she let her mask fall, compelled to be truthful with him. "I don't normally connect with strangers. I don't know how to explain this . . . bonding with you, and that bothers me too."

He took her hand. She was surprised at his gesture. For a moment she felt a shiver race through her, as if by his voluntarily touching her, he'd given his approval to their connection. For a moment she allowed herself to simply look at him, be with him, to acknowledge the confusion she felt, to register the promise of desire between them. No man's presence had ever unsettled her before as this one's did.

He blinked and gave a slight shake of his head as if he, too, was caught up in the moment. *Good.* She was glad to know that he was as bothered as she. At least part of her plan was working.

Rasch turned her small hand over in his large one and examined it. His fingers encountered the well-callused palm, and he pursed his lips. "Ah, Lady, you are a mystery that I shall have to solve. You bring out something primitive in me, something I'm not quite certain I understand. Are you truly all-seeing?"

No, she wanted to say, but the disturbing current of desire was there, ever present between them. Her pulse sang, and her skin heated beneath his touch. Something was happening between them, something she hadn't intended and couldn't control. She pulled her hand away, no longer trusting herself in such proximity to him.

Maybe this was not a good idea. Maybe she should have heeded Niko's warning not to do this. But she had to be the one to punish the judge; otherwise her father would do it himself. He was too old, and the risks too great.

The plan had seemed so easy. She didn't have to do anything except make the judge fall in love with her. And without knowing it, he was already halfway there, she felt sure. But she'd never considered that her own heart might be in danger, or that the bewitched could be so bewitching.

She knew now that he'd take her along on his journey. She let out a measured sigh. She would have ten days to fulfill her vow. Ten days to destroy Judge Horatio Webber, the man who'd killed her brother.

The bells around Savannah's ankle jingled merrily as they left the café. Climbing into the compact truck, she gave Rasch a conspiratorial smile, tossed her head, and sent her rich black hair flying in the crisp mountain air.

"Thank you for the food, Crusader. Perhaps sometime I'll cook for you in return."

"I think you ought to know that I don't like mushrooms, and poisoned apples are out of vogue. Besides, what about the friend you said you're meeting?"

"One never knows about friends. That's why I filled my pockets with junk food and bread crumbs," she quipped. "If I'm abandoned, I have food. If I get lost, I'll follow my trail of bread crumbs through the woods."

"A regular Girl Scout," Rasch responded with an answering laugh. "Be prepared."

Suddenly the day seemed a lot brighter. The drive was quiet and private. The small truck hugged the side of the mountain as they wound their way up it. Only occasionally did they pass another automobile or camper. They continued to climb, looping back and forth like a ribbon across the side of the forest as they rose. With every mile Rasch seemed more relaxed, and there was a feeling of silent camaraderie building between them. She'd wanted to capture his interest and make him accept her, but it had been accomplished too easily. It didn't make sense. Instead of feeling pleased, Savannah found herself becoming increasingly uneasy.

"Where will you camp?" she finally asked.

"I haven't decided yet. There are shelters along the trail, but there are usually several people bedding down in each lean-to. I like my privacy, so I usually find a spot in the woods and sleep under the stars. What about you?"

"I don't know. But under the stars sounds good to me. Tell me about the trail."

"Why?"

"Because I'd like to know, and it pleases me to hear your voice. I told you that I like sounds. Sounds help me know where I am."

"Like a physical roadmap?"

"Physical, yes. And emotional, too, I think. Why, is that a problem for you? Had you rather I not speak?"

"No," he admitted, "I think I rather like your voice. I'm not accustomed to having someone around. Usually I come up here alone."

"And I'm a distraction that you'd rather not deal with?"

"Not at all. I'd rather deal with you, but you seem to come close for a second, then just when I'm about to get some kind of fix on you, you move away in some new direction."

"I do?" She leaned forward, her bells jingling as she moved.

"Well, maybe you don't move, exactly, it's more that you disintegrate and reassemble in some new place. You're like a novel of suspense. What seems to be real is in fact not real at all."

"A novel of suspense? You mean a horror novel?" She pretended to be seriously put out. "If you must fictionalize me, couldn't I be a novel of fantasy?"

"Why?"

"In fantasy what is real continues to be real until you believe that it isn't."

"And are you real?" he asked, his deep voice seductive.

She looked out the window for a moment, catching sight of a hawk curling across the valley below. "I'm real, Crusader. I'm very real."

Abruptly Rasch switched on the radio, twisting the dial back and forth as the sound of static chattered in the silence. Sighing resignedly, he gave up and turned it off.

"I think that you might enjoy camping out on

Nightshadow Ridge," he remarked, trying to keep the conversation light.

She twisted around in her seat, planting her back against the door so that she could study him. She needed to look at him, to ground herself in his reality in order to carry out her own plans. Their conversation was too comfortable, she reflected, too pleasant. Her plan to intrigue and ensnare him appeared to be working, but there was danger in letting herself enjoy his company too much.

She let her eyes explore the man beside her. Not only was he ruggedly handsome and sensual, beneath the surface there was some inner force that intimidated and confused her.

Savannah tucked her foot beneath her, watching as Rasch absently rubbed the spot beneath his right ear. His lips narrowed into a frown. She was tempted to reach out and reassure him, but checked herself. She didn't understand the attraction she felt for the man she'd sworn to punish.

"Are there ghosts?" she asked, trying to shake off the feeling.

"On Nightshadow Ridge? Possibly. But they've never shown themselves to me. With you along, the forest ranger will probably have to send out a call for ghostbusters if the other campers are going to get any sleep. I have the feeling you attract spirits."

Savannah didn't think the presence of ghosts would keep her awake nearly as much as the presence of the man beside her. By now, any ordinary man would either have bombarded her with questions or opened the truck door and asked her to leave. Horatio Webber seemed to understand, as much as she, that they were engaged in some kind of predestined spiritual joining and had better let it play itself out.

She'd set out to plant the suggestion of herself in his mind. The only special power she had was her imagination. She'd tempt him, mystify him, tantalize him both physically and mentally, so that by the time they met, he'd be intrigued. She thought he was. But so was *she*!

Perhaps this growing mutual awareness that wasn't part of her plan had its advantages though. Physical attraction wouldn't be enough. She would have to attract this man on all levels. Savannah was beginning to realize that he never did anything halfway. If her plan was to work, she would have to captivate him body, mind, and soul.

Suddenly Savannah remembered Zeena's admonishment that she was opening a Pandora's box and that nobody could predict what would happen when she did. Zeena never told the future of those who lived in the circus. She refused to look. Still, sometimes an expression crossed Zeena's face that said she knew more than she told. And Savannah knew that Zeena hadn't wanted her to leave the troupe's permanent quarters. She had disregarded Zeena's warning to let it be.

If the judge had refused her request for a ride, she'd have pretended to be helpless, desperate, flirtatious even. What she hadn't expected was that he'd be so agreeable. Nor had she anticipated his response to her on an intellectual level, or her own awareness of him. His mind reached out to her, and she felt herself falling into an easy intimacy that surprised her.

Savannah hadn't told her father where she was

going. Alfred Ramey was accustomed to his children going off on their own, and he never insisted on knowing their plans. That was why it had been so easy for Tifton to conceal his arrest and jail sentence, why it was too late by the time Savannah had received his call for help. Tifton was already dead, killed by a cellmate, in a jail where he'd been sent by Judge Horatio Webber.

But Judge Webber was proving to be an enigma. By reputation he was a man who stood firm, a man who stood for probity and made no compromises. She knew from both research and personal experience that nothing could sway him once he'd made up his mind. His deafness to Tifton's appeal for leniency was proof of that.

Tifton, in his naïveté, hadn't considered the consequences of his actions. He believed that the judge, like everyone else in his life, would fall victim to his charm and accept his story that it wasn't his fault; that it was all a mistake. Tifton exaggerated when it suited his purposes, but he didn't lie. Nevertheless, Judge Webber weighed the facts and made the decision to make an example of Tifton. And then Tifton was dead.

"You know my name," Savannah said quietly. "What shall I call you?"

"My friends call me Rasch."

"Is that what I am—a friend?"

"No, I don't think so. I'm not yet sure what you are."

"Then until you decide, I shall call you Crusader. And you shall call me Savannah, for that's how I'm known by everyone."

"Then everyone is your friend?"

"No," she answered, "not everyone. I, too, have enemies."

Rasch heard the hint of bitterness in her voice. He could identify with that; he, too, felt animosity toward the people who wished him harm. But this darkly beautiful woman? What enemies could she possibly have? Was there a jealous lover in her past, or perhaps a woman whose lover she'd stolen?

No, that seemed wrong. Her beauty undoubtedly enchanted other women's lovers, but without any intention on her part to beguile them. She exuded an integrity that suggested she would find all meanness and cruelty abhorrent. She was like a statue he'd seen in a museum. From one side the porcelain figure was strong and pure. Viewed from the other side, her lips were tinged with pain, and her eyes stared with unseeing weariness.

"I think I'll call you Gypsy," Rasch remarked. "It suits a woman of mystery and intrigue."

Savannah shivered. He was too close to the truth. She glanced out the window and saw how the land fell sharply away from the road, cutting into a chasm of sky that seemed endless. They were so high that a cloud of fog shielded the bottom until they came to a spot where the valley below spread out below like an orange-and-yellow Chinese silk fan.

"It's beautiful here," she whispered.

"Yes."

But Rasch's words were not in response to the panorama of the valley below, but the raw beauty of the woman who shared his vision.

Once again he wondered who she was, and what she planned to do. That she'd stalked him was obvious. She'd gone to some trouble to appear on his balcony. Next she'd beckoned to him in the smoky street only to disappear before he could reach her. Then she'd resurfaced in the lights of his truck on a deserted road, miles away from Atlanta.

Rasch was a keen observer of people; he'd had years of experience as a judge to hone his powers of perception. She was definitely stalking him, and he couldn't recall when he'd been more fascinated. He wanted very much to know what Savannah really wanted from him.

He'd accepted her ploy that she needed a ride. He'd known that she was manipulating him when he bought the boots and clothing. She obviously knew nothing about hiking, and he'd long since decided that she was alone. There would be no friends waiting at the park, just as there was probably no friend being sent for help for the disabled truck, if indeed it was disabled.

A judge was always on the alert for malcontents, for the disgruntled victims of the legal system intent on getting even, but after a quick search of her gear when he was stowing their goods, he hadn't found any weapons. She was up to something; he just didn't know what. He surprised even himself by his decision to play along. Sooner or later he'd learn what she wanted, then he'd decide what action to take.

For now he allowed himself to be caught up in her spell. She'd come to him out of the mists with nothing except a meager backpack. Surely all of this couldn't be an attempt to seduce him. He was no stranger to women. He could be enticed into bed without any elaborate charade so long as the woman understood the ground rules of his life: no promises, no involvement, no future.

Rasch Webber had set a course for his life that didn't include the distraction of marriage and a family. A man had to channel all his energies toward his goals, and Rasch had found in the law an all-consuming career. Nor did he seek to unburden his innermost secrets to a wife. Rasch alone knew that he'd survived a dreadful childhood by reading about Superman and other action heroes who believed in justice and truth. As a small boy, viewing the world from the section of town where pimps and drug dealers were the role models, he'd made up his mind that one day he'd be one of the good guys he read about. And Gypsy? What was she?

A voyager, that was the name Savannah had given herself, a woman on a quest. He could believe that even if he didn't know what she was seeking, or understand her ability to communicate with animals. He didn't know much about the so-called new-age beliefs. He only knew there was something mysteriously Old World about his passenger.

Yes, the name Gypsy suited her better than Savannah.

Still, Rasch would bet his last dollar that she was more in touch with the present than with the future, or the past. There was a shimmering vibrancy about her that was almost tangible. Her lithe body, with firm, full breasts and slim but curvaceous hips caused a stirring deep in his loins, and her stunning face, with its sultry beauty, mesmerized his attention.

Catching her full lower lip between perfect white teeth, she glanced over the incline. "Are we going higher, Crusader?"

"Oh, yes. The park and the start of the trail are just ahead. Once we check in and register our destination, it will be midday. I plan to move on to the top of the ridge before camping for the night. Others prefer to sleep in the facility at the falls provided for trail walkers, and get an early start the next morning."

"Getting started early suits me fine too. I'm eager to get on the trail," Savannah told him.

"Ah, but what about your friend? He—or she— might not agree."

"Then I'll go alone."

"That wouldn't be a good idea, Savannah. It isn't safe on a trail for a woman alone, even an experienced camper. The rangers prefer that hikers go in pairs."

"But they can't physically stop me, can they?"

"No, I suppose not, unless you're drinking, or there is some potential for physical or legal liability."

"That's what I thought," Savannah replied with a Mona Lisa smile.

Rasch parked in the designated area and helped Savannah from the truck as he looked expectantly around. There were no friends waiting for Savannah, just as Rasch had suspected. "Looks like there's only us."

"Looks that way."

The ranger on duty came out on the porch and greeted them. "Hi. It's been a while, Rasch. Who's your friend?" He glanced down at Savannah's bare feet and lifted his eyebrows in amusement.

"Her truck broke down a ways back. She plans to hike the trail."

"This part of the trail is pretty rough. Have you walked it before?"

"Er, no." Savannah followed the ranger and Rasch inside. She was beginning to get a sinking feeling that her plans were about to fall apart, just when success had seemed imminent.

"That probably isn't a smart idea, ma'am, not even for an experienced camper. Maybe you ought to join a group."

"Thank you for your concern," Savannah said, her voice soft but determined, "but I can make it. Where do I sign?"

The ranger indicated the register signed by all those walking the Appalachian Trail. There was a place for time of departure, destination, and expected time of arrival. By keeping such a record, the authorities could sound the alarm if anyone failed to show up in due time.

Rasch had hung back, letting Savannah struggle with her lie. He decided that he'd punished her long enough. Now he stepped forward. "Never mind, Paul, I'll look after her. She can come with me."

The ranger looked relieved. "Well, that's good of you, Rasch. What's the plan?"

"I'm going to meet Jake at Bly Gap and drive on into Asheville. Should take about ten days." He filled in the log.

The ranger turned the page and handed it to Savannah for her signature. "And you?"

"The same. Thank you for your concern, Ranger. The judge says that Nightshadow Ridge is a good place to camp."

The ranger gave Rasch an odd look as he replaced the register on the counter. He assembled the usual camping brochures and maps and handed them to Savannah. "Well, I hope the weather stays good for you. Glad to have you, Ms."—he glanced back at the register—"Ms.—"

"Savannah." Savannah cut the ranger off, stuffed the papers into her backpack, and started up the trail with more determination than sense of direction.

"Wait, Savannah," Rasch called out. "If you're traveling with me, I lead—that is, if you think you can keep up."

"I can go anywhere you go," she said, and he knew that she would.

There was no challenge in her voice, simply a statement of fact. He nodded and started up the trail, setting a fast pace. She watched him, allowing herself to notice the graceful way he moved, the confidence, the sheer physical beauty of the man. How could he be so appealing and yet be her enemy?

Walking in the woods, feeling the warmth of the sun, listening to the sound of Rasch's jeans rustling crisply as he walked, made it easy to imagine how glorious this time together could be if things were different, if they were just a man and his ladylove out for an afternoon promenade.

They walked along in silence for a while before Rasch slowed his pace and spoke. "Talk to me, Savannah. Tell me what interests you other than chipmunks and a crusty old loner like me."

Savannah frowned. "You're not old. A little crusty, maybe, but hardly a curmudgeon. I like honest people who work hard and try to make the world better in some way." People like you, she mused, then wished the thought hadn't slipped into her mind.

"I agree about making the world better," Rasch

said, "but I'm afraid that I see fewer and fewer people trying to accomplish that."

"Maybe you aren't looking hard enough."

"I'm looking, they just aren't there."

Though Rasch had slowed down, he still moved along at a steady clip. Savannah tried to follow without breathing heavily, but her ears were popping. She opened her mouth wide and closed it again, trying to rid herself of the full feeling that had settled in her head.

"Here, try some of this." Rasch stopped, pulled a pack of gum out of his pocket and handed it to her.

She took it, glancing at the brand with a smile. "Red-hot cinnamon? Somehow I'd have guessed that you were a wintergreen man, or perhaps peppermint."

"Just proves that looks can be deceiving," he said, and gave her a smile that tore at the protective cover with which she'd so carefully insulated herself.

"My sentiment exactly," she managed to say as she unwrapped the stick of gum and popped it into her mouth.

"Unwrap one for me, too, will you?"

Unwrapping the gum wasn't a problem, but putting it between his lips and sliding it into his mouth was an experiment in self-control. When his lips brushed the end of her fingertips, she felt the current flare between them. She drew back and looked quickly away, her cheeks warm, her heart pumping wildly. What was happening?

"Thanks," Rasch said, his voice oddly low.

She could feel his eyes on her for a long moment, then he turned his attention back to the trail, this time picking up his rapid pace again, as if he were in a hurry to get somewhere, or away from somewhere.

By the time he stopped again, for water and a snack of trail mix, it was late afternoon, and Savannah's emotions were strung as tight as the high wire on which she and Tifton had performed for so many years. *Tifton*. She closed her eyes and took a deep breath, trying desperately to focus on Tifton and her reason for being alone on this mountain with the man she'd sworn to punish. So far, the only one being punished appeared to be herself.

Savannah knew that she had nine and a half days left.

She had nine and a half days to make Judge Horatio Webber need her.

Nine and a half days to give this stranger love . . . and then vanish from his life forever.

Three

Savannah slid out of the straps of her backpack and plopped down on a tree stump. She could hear the rush of water somewhere in the thick growth of rhododendrons beyond the trail. In the spring this would be a fairyland. Now it was dotted with confetti-colored leaves and pine straw, like some crazy quilt of red and orange and brown.

"We have about another hour's walk," Rasch said. "That is, if you still think you can keep up with me."

"Of course I can," she answered, and pushed herself quickly to her feet. Suddenly she felt as if she were touching the ground after having been in the air for hours, practicing, rehearsing, pushing herself and Tifton to new heights. After a particularly daring move there was always a moment of disorientation when the thrill subsided and reality intruded again.

Suddenly Rasch was beside her, holding her by

both elbows, peering into her eyes. "Are you all right?"

She raised her eyelids and caught the concentration of his gaze. For just a moment she felt the weakness intensify. She closed her eyes, fighting off the dizzying effect of his nearness, and took a deep breath.

"I'm fine. It's the altitude, I guess."

"Don't you like heights?"

He thought she had acrophobia? If the situation weren't so ridiculous, she'd laugh. She, one half of the Flying Gypsies trapeze act, afraid of heights? Still, for now it was important that he not suspect who she was.

"It isn't that," she said slowly. "For some reason I feel a bit light-headed. Just give me a moment to find my mountain-climbing legs, and I'll be as ready as you."

Ready? That was a phrase with which Rasch could identify. Right here, in the wilderness, with a woman he didn't know, he was as ready as he'd ever been. But what he was ready for wasn't climbing mountains, or trading heated touches, or fishing for information. It took every ounce of willpower he possessed to release this highly desirable woman and step away from her.

"Better put on those jeans and boots," he said sharply. "Climbing a mountain barefoot in a skirt isn't the best way to travel."

"I'll be fine," she said automatically. Removing her clothes now was an action she didn't even want to consider.

"Well, if you step on a snake, don't say I didn't warn

you." Rasch picked up her knapsack and held it while she threaded her arms through the straps.

"Snakes don't scare me."

"What does scare you, Savannah?"

"People," she replied immediately. "People hurt more people than animals ever will."

Rasch frowned. Savannah could be so open, so forthright—he liked this aspect of her—and yet she hid so much of herself from his scrutiny. He wanted to know all of her, dammit . . . he wanted to know her in every sense of the word, in every fiber of her being.

"Let's go." His voice was gruff, and he knew that he was being unreasonable by not giving her more time to get used to the altitude.

Savannah forced herself to allow Rasch to adjust the placement of the straps on her backpack, his fingertips setting off pinwheels of sensation. Any more touching, and she wouldn't have to do *any* climbing. She could attach herself to him magnetically and be carried along.

"Do you know a lot about snakes?" she asked, as much to cover her confusion as to make conversation.

"Enough, I suppose. Why, are you on speaking terms with them too?"

Savannah shrugged her shoulders, trying to get the backpack arranged comfortably. "I really don't talk to animals. At least not consciously. It's a mental thing."

"Well, let's hope that you speak mental bear, too, because we're in bear country up here, and I didn't bring my gun." Rasch took a long look at Savannah, then shook his head before he turned and started off through the woods. He was satisfied with her knapsack, but her dress still bothered him. It wasn't so much that her attire was inappropriate as that it was distracting to him. Or perhaps it was the graceful curves of her femininity that were so disconcerting.

"Bears? Do you think we'll meet any?"

"After what's happened to me in the last twenty-four hours, nothing would surprise me, Savannah."

Rasch pushed a limb away and held it back for Savannah to precede him. She drew even, stopped, and looked at him for a long moment, then passed by, her skirt swishing against his legs like feathers. He fell in behind her, allowing her to lead the way. The occasional trill of her ankle bracelet echoed through the trees as if it were speaking a language of its own.

They climbed steadily for a time, listening to the lyrical sound of the mountain stream in the distance. The late afternoon heat enveloped them, and perspiration dripped down Rasch's forehead. It was October, for God's sake, not the middle of June, but the damp, humid air created steam.

Ahead, Savannah seemed little touched by the climate. There were leaves and puff-ball seeds caught in her dark hair. Her feet, sure and certain, moved lightly along the trail. She appeared to have gotten her second wind as she stepped over logs and debris, as if she knew where they were going and was eager to arrive.

Then suddenly she stopped.

Rasch stumbled, barely halting before he plowed into her. "What's wrong?"

"Listen," she said softly.

"I'm listening. What am I supposed to hear?"

"That's what I mean. The woods are silent. Where

are the animal sounds?" There was no movement, no sound, not even the rustling of the leaves.

"I can't say. You're the spiritualist, you tell me. Can't you call up your guide and ask him to take a little look-see?"

"I don't have a guide," Savannah retorted crossly. She hadn't intended for her aura of mystery to go so far. Now even she was getting prickly feelings that made spider movements down her backbone. "We're being watched."

"I think you're right," Rasch agreed, casting his eyes in a slow arc around the woods. "Any suggestions?"

"Just be quiet."

Savannah eased her backpack from her shoulders, kneeling as it slid to the ground. "Why don't we rest a bit, maybe have a candy bar?"

"Candy bar? You have candy bars?"

"Yes. In my pocket with the bread crumbs, and some other goodies."

"What else do you have hidden away that I don't know about?"

"Aha! You don't expect me to tell you all my secrets, do you?"

"Absolutely. And I don't intend to wait much longer, Gypsy. You owe me some truths, remember?" Rasch started to slip his backpack from his shoulders.

"No, don't do that. Just move past me up the trail and wait."

Rasch caught the warning in her voice, and surprised himself by complying without question.

"I think that we'll leave this pack of vanilla wafers

behind, as a kind of peace offering for the creatures of the forest."

She stared off into the trees for a long moment, removed the wrapper, and laid the cookies on a flat rock. With a confident smile she walked up the trail to where Rasch was waiting.

"I don't suppose that our visitor sent you a telepathic message that it's a cookie monster, did it?"

"No, it didn't send me any message at all."

"And I thought you communicated with the animals."

"Let's not talk about that anymore. Animals don't understand words, but they can pick up on our fear. How much farther to our campsite?" Savannah's voice was almost singsong light.

"Not far."

Rasch might be willing to play her mystery game, but he didn't know who they were playing with, and if their watcher wasn't an animal, he certainly didn't want to divulge their campsite to whoever was listening.

Savannah swished her skirts, shaking out imaginary wrinkles, turned around, and motioned for Rasch to lead the way. At the top of the incline she stopped, touched his shoulder, and pointed back at the rock, visible from where they were standing. The cookies were gone.

The birds had begun to sing, and the normal sounds of the forest returned. Rasch was supposed to be protecting her. He hated to admit that his companion had sensed something that he missed. Normally he would have noticed the silence and been concerned. Today all he could think about was his mysterious Gypsy. The sound of her voice and the music of her bells were all his ears had heard.

"You know what happens when you feed a stray animal," Rasch growled. "They expect it."

"Whatever was back there is just as wary of us as you were of it."

"What was it?"

Savannah made an impatient sound. "Crusader, you may be the most prolific interrogator of all time."

"I just like to know what I'm dealing with. And I think that you like to create mystery, Gypsy. Who, or what, was there?"

"A bear, perhaps, or maybe some other wild animal. I'm not sure."

"I suppose you just got a message that it was hungry."

"No, I didn't get any message at all. I just knew it was there, as you did."

"I didn't know anything until you made us stop and listen. If it didn't communicate with you, how did you know?"

"The animals grew quiet. The woods were too still. There were little sounds that moved with us and stopped when we did. I wasn't certain, of course, but I thought that something was walking with us."

"Savannah, I've walked these woods for fifteen years, and outside of other campers, and a couple of hunters, I've never seen anything that wasn't more afraid of me than I was of it."

"You haven't looked. Remember what Hamlet said—how does it go? 'There are more things in heaven and earth than are dreamt of in your philosophy, Horatio'?"

"I don't know. If it isn't in a law book, I probably haven't read it."

"That's your problem, Crusader, you travel much too narrow a line. It won't work, you know. People aren't always what they seem, and you, I think, are lying to yourself. Good and evil make up the world, but they aren't so clearly divided as that."

"You're not a psychic, or a voyager, my lady of mystery—you're a philosopher after all."

"No, I'm a human being, composed of both good and evil, just like you, Judge Horatio Webber. Maybe it's time you learned. Maybe I'll be the one to teach you how to find the truth."

"Maybe, Gypsy, but you could be wrong. Have you ever considered how much happier the world would be if a thing were either right or wrong, if people were simply good or bad, if everything were clearly one thing or the other?"

There was such pain in his voice. She almost reached out and touched him. For just a moment she wanted to reassure him, tell him that she understood. Had she misjudged him? Was he caught up in some terrible event over which he'd lost control?

No, she told herself sternly. He knew what he was doing. She couldn't allow her growing awareness of the man to weaken her will. Women were always drawn to the wrong men. She simply had to toughen her resolve.

Rasch reached the top of the ridge and stopped, waiting for Savannah to join him. Beyond the trees, shimmering in the late afternoon sun, was Shadow Lake, clear and green and peaceful. On the other side of the lake was an abandoned cabin that Rasch had used on occasion when he wanted to get out of the rain or the cold, but he wouldn't pass that on to his companion just yet. She'd wanted to tag along, and she might as well face the rigors that accompanied camping out.

Savannah came to a stop beside him and took a deep breath. "It's beautiful, but a little lonely."

"Yes, it's lonely because it's supposed to be haunted by a beautiful young Indian maiden who threw herself into the lake when she was told that her lover was dead."

"Yes. This is a sad place, but it isn't evil."

"No? Well, I've never had any problems. But I've never had a Gypsy woman along with me either. Perhaps I'm tempting fate."

"Tempting fate?" Savannah's voice quivered. She placed her hand on Rasch's arm, more a gesture of denial than of disbelief.

Rasch looked down at her. He couldn't fathom the veiled look in her dark eyes. She seemed to be seeing something that he couldn't see. There was a hint of the same sadness that he'd sensed in her on the patio and later in the street. Regret mixed with fear and anguish washed across her face.

"Don't worry, Gypsy," he said softly. "I'll protect you. I take my duties seriously. I won't let anything happen, I promise."

"Don't make any rash promises, Crusader. A crusader can never be sure of the consequences of his actions. A crusader never knows how much he can hurt in the name of doing good."

The sun dropped behind the mountain across the lake, and the wind skipped across the water, ruffling the surface and obliterating the reflection of the sky.

"We'd better set up camp," Rasch said, prying her fingers from his arm and clasping them between his own. Her hand was cold, but warmed as their fingers intertwined. He could feel the erratic beat of her pulse, the tension as she pulled away.

"Savannah? What's wrong?"

She stopped and swung around to face him. "More questions, Crusader? What do you want from me?"

"I want—" Then, as he looked down at her, he felt the magnetic current arc between them, saw the distress in her eyes mutate into something less fearful but more confusing. At that moment he knew what he wanted, and he lowered his head, expecting her to cry out and run away.

She didn't move. Instead, Savannah waited, her heart pounding, her emotions warring with her mind, her body singing with a song that was deceptively enticing.

Their lips met, brushed, drew back, and claimed each other again. Cold became hot. Solid became liquid. Control became release. And Savannah felt as if she were sweeping through the air, through currents that seared and churned, then flung her into space.

Nothing in her past could compare with the sensations that flowed between her and the man who was kissing her. They stood, touching only their lips and fingertips, until Rasch abruptly wrenched his mouth from hers and stepped away. He lifted her hand, examined it as if it were some precious object to be treasured, then released it as though his fingers were dissolving away from hers.

"I don't understand," he said simply.

Savannah turned away. Everything was going according to plan; he was falling into her trap . . . but she hadn't intended to be caught in the spell as well.

Should she call it all off, forget the whole plan? She'd been so sure that what she was doing was right. She'd force him to lower his defenses and let her in. Then, when he was most vulnerable, she'd strike. Stealing his heart had been her goal. Now she was confused. Her resolve was wavering, as if she'd lost touch with her purpose. Everything seemed muted, less defined, like a pastel drawing all smudged and soft.

All she could say was "Neither do I." She whirled and dashed down the ridge toward the edge of the lake. Her rapid movements made the ankle bracelet chime merrily. The wind picked up the sound and carried it across the lake, kissed the hillside with the music, and flung it back again.

To Rasch, the soft reverberation could have been laughter.

To Savannah, it sounded like crying.

After a long moment Rasch followed her. He reached her side at the water's edge and set her to gathering dead limbs and brush to build a fire. He found rocks that he used to circle the fire site. After the wood started to blaze, he began to assemble the small tent he'd unpacked.

"You're going to sleep in that?" Savannah asked as she dropped another armful of branches.

"*We're* going to sleep in this."

"We? Isn't it pretty small," she asked skeptically.

"I didn't expect to share it." He secured the last stake.

"You won't have to. I have my own sleeping bag. I'll be just fine out here by the fire."

"Whatever you say. But it gets pretty spooky out here at night, and cold too."

"I'll manage. I'm used to sleeping beneath the stars."

He shrugged. "Then let's get your bedroll out now. I like to have the camp set up before dark."

Savannah untied her pack and laid it out, stuffing her clothing into a pillowcase and laying it aside. Her extra candy bars, trail mix, and other food was already tied in a waterproof drawstring bag. She looked around for a tree from which to hang it, as Niko had instructed.

"Here, I'll take that and hang it with mine." Rasch took both parcels and walked back to the tree line. Looping a rope over a limb, he tied both bags away from the ground.

By the time he unfolded his sleeping bag and arranged it inside the tent, the sun had dropped behind the mountain.

Savannah shivered and moved closer to the fire. Rasch was right. The air coming off the water was cold. She regretted not changing into the jeans and shirt as he'd suggested. But a show of weakness would be a mistake now.

"What are we cooking?" she asked, trying to conceal the chattering of her teeth.

"Fill the cook pot with water from the lake," he instructed as he began to remove foil packets from his cache of supplies.

Savannah took the pot and knelt at the edge of the water, hoping that the water she'd scooped up was clear. As she stood there, fog snaked across the valley, closing out the last of the sun. Little tags of vapor drifted up from the water, merging with the wisps of clouds. In the distance the mountains took on the color that gave them their name, the Blue Ridge Mountains.

The sound of her anklet bells sounded faint as she danced back to the fire. Suddenly Savannah wasn't brave anymore. *Think about Tifton*, she told herself. *Remember why you're here*. She tried hard to concentrate on seeing her laughing, blue-eyed brother, to remember him walking the wire in his blue satin costume. But for the first time, even the sound of his laughter escaped her.

It was this sad location. Never had she been in a place that seemed so unstable. The ground didn't move, but all the elements above it shifted and blurred in the night air. The only solid force in her vicinity was Rasch Webber. She looked for him, finding him staring at her with an odd expression on his face, as if he, too, were trying to bring something to mind.

"Wow! Crusader," she managed to say, "when you said there were spirits, you didn't exaggerate, did you?"

Rasch heard the uncertainty in her voice and felt some regret. He, too, had always felt uncomfortable by the lake after the sun went down. His custom was to come here during the day to fish, but then to move his campsite farther up the mountain on the opposite side.

But tonight was different. He hadn't noticed the quiet unease. Tonight was filled with his Gypsy and the magic of her presence.

"It's likely some of your spirits, Gypsy. Can't you say some magic words to let them know we're friendly?"

"Are we, Crusader? Friendly, I mean?" She drew her gaze away as she answered her own question. Lovers they would become, but to be friends with the man responsible for her brother's death? That was the last thing she wanted.

"I don't know, you'll have to tell me."

Savannah gave her skirts a little shake and jutted her chin forward. She didn't want to make him more suspicious than he already was. "Of course we are," she said brightly. "And I'm hungry. What goes in the water?"

"First you're going to pour part of the water into this coffeepot. Then we're going to bring the rest to a boil for stew."

"Stew?"

"Dehydrated. Tonight I'll make it easy on you. Tomorrow we catch our own dinner. That lake is full of fish."

"Wonderful." Savannah sank down, folding her legs beneath her Indian-style. Her skirt covered her feet and warmed them, but her arms were soon speckled with chill bumps.

"Are you cold?" Rasch asked, hiding a smile behind a genuine concern. "Why don't you change clothes?"

"I'm fine," Savannah insisted, determined not to let him know the extent of her discomfort. Soon her front was warmed by the campfire. But her back was chilled to the bone.

By the time the water boiled and Rasch poured the hot coffee into collapsible tin cups, Savannah was so cold that she would have drunk the hot water without the coffee.

"Umm, this is good, Crusader. What kind of stew are we having?"

"It's beef and it's hot, so be careful that you don't burn your tongue." He handed her a cup of the steaming meat.

The stew was surprisingly good. Had Savannah been the cook, she could have improved it with the addition of a few herbs she'd noticed back on the trail, but she was too hungry to quibble. Starting tomorrow, she'd take over as chef.

When they finished eating, Rasch took the cups and spoons down to the water and rinsed them. Afterward, he collapsed them and replaced them in his backpack. "I always keep my supplies packed," he explained, "in case I have to move out quickly."

"Move out?" Savannah glanced around.

"In case of bears," he said casually, feeling ashamed of himself even as he spoke. He'd seen an occasional panhandling bear along the trail, but they weren't aggressive. Still, he didn't know what had eaten the vanilla wafers. The worst problem he'd ever encountered were the sudden rainstorms that came up. Occasional snowflakes he could take, even the cold, but the rain could come quick and heavy. Rain had sent him scurrying around the lake to seek out the abandoned cabin more than once. No point in letting Savannah know anything about that—not just yet—not until he learned what she was up to.

As they sat by the fire, Savannah watched the mist rising from the water and tried to understand her unease.

Rasch watched Savannah, studying her proud profile against the light from the fire. Something about the faraway look in her eyes almost forbade conversation, but he couldn't tear his gaze from her enchanting features.

"Who are you, Gypsy?" he heard himself ask.

"Is it important for you to know?"

He thought about her question. Yesterday, last week, even this morning, who she was would have been important. Now? Perhaps it wasn't. Perhaps knowing would spoil the illusion, and he had so few illusions left about life and the people he met.

Whatever she was, or wasn't, would be the same tomorrow. Tonight, for a reason he couldn't begin to understand, he wouldn't force her to strip the veils of mystery away.

"No," he finally answered, "I suppose not. What about you? Aren't you in the least concerned about me? Suppose I were an ax murderer? I could do bad things to you and nobody would ever know."

She laughed lightly. "Are you? I should think a judge would have more efficient ways to get rid of people he considered undesirable."

"That's a strange way to describe what I do—get rid of people."

"Well, isn't that accurate? I mean, you put them in jail, but do you really know what happens to the people you sentence?"

"No, not always. All I'm expected to do is interpret the law. My sentences are carried out by others."

"So if someone you sentence is murdered, you would never know it. Doesn't that bother you, making decisions about life and death?"

Not know? Oh, yes, there were times when he knew—when the story of a murder made the front pages of the newspaper. Had she read about the Tifton Ramey case as well? He took a long time before answering. "Sometimes I know, and it bothers me. There are times when justice isn't served no matter what I do."

"But you pronounce your sentences anyway, heedless of the consequences, don't you?"

"It's my job. And I do it because I'm a man who's very tired of bad people doing bad things to good people."

"Sometimes good people do bad things to good people too. Don't they?"

"Yes, but not often, thank God."

This time Savannah couldn't hold back a shiver.

Rasch looked at his watch. It wasn't even eight o'clock, but he knew that Savannah had to be tired from their long hike, and he knew, too, that she was cold, in spite of her protests to the contrary.

"I'm about ready to turn in, Gypsy, how about you?"

Savannah looked at the bedroll and the fire. She was certainly exhausted, and half frozen, and she couldn't sit up all night. "Yes, I suppose. Shall I pile some more wood on the fire first?"

"I'll get another load before we turn in," Rasch agreed cheerfully, too cheerfully. He felt the way he had once as a teenager when three of his buddies had convinced their girls to accompany them on a camping trip. The boys' plans hadn't been innocent, but after trying half the night to get up the nerve to talk the girls into sharing their sleeping bags, they'd chickened out at dawn and gone home, hungry, tired, and disappointed.

"Good." Savannah could have told him that she

could forage for wood, build and maintain a campfire as good as he, but she was glad to have a few minutes away from him. He hadn't sounded as if he'd enjoyed sentencing people. He probably never even knew that he'd been responsible for poor Tifton's death. Well, sooner or later he'd know. Savannah would see to that.

For now she badly needed to get some sleep. The day's activities had left her nervous system in shambles. And it wasn't just the cold that was making her shiver.

"You ought to find yourself a bush while I'm gone," the judge called out. "Then take off those clothes before you climb into that bag."

"What?" She couldn't keep the incredulousness from her voice.

"Well, it's a long time until morning, and you never know about the bears."

Bears and bushes weren't what was suddenly occupying Savannah's mind. Take off her clothes? What did the man think she was, some kind of exhibitionist? Still, he had a point about the bushes, and she scurried to take care of the situation, dashing back to the fire by the time he returned. As Rasch dropped part of the wood on the fire and piled the rest nearby, she zipped open her bag and brushed off her feet as she stepped inside and sat down.

"Suit yourself," Rasch said casually, "but after you've hiked all day, even Gypsy clothes are sweaty, dirty. It isn't healthy to sleep in them. Most campers sleep in sweatsuits, or—nothing at all."

He wasn't emphasizing the "nothing at all" as a personal challenge. Intellectually she knew he was right. Emotionally she fought every thought that slid unbidden into her mind, every thought of Rasch Webber sleeping in the buff and herself lying naked beside him.

"I'm not a person who sleeps nude," she said, her voice taut as she fought the breathlessness that had attacked her vocal cords. She slid down in the bag and zipped herself inside. *Certainly not now, not tonight, not with you.*

"The nymph on my balcony was nude."

"I was not—" The words just slipped out. Savannah could have bitten her tongue off. She waited for Rasch to say something, anything. But he didn't. He just stared at her from where he was standing beside the fire. The flickering light threw shadows across his stern face, darkening gray eyes that seemed to bore holes through her. She hadn't been nude. She'd been wearing a flesh-colored body suit.

Savannah shivered and snuggled lower in the bag. *He's caught you in his trap like one of those criminals he deals with,* she thought, *and you can't even begin to run.*

"Good night, Gypsy," he finally said, forcing himself to look away, cutting off the tension that flashed between them like summer lightning.

There was a rumble from somewhere deep in the mountains, and the sound came morose and eerie across the water. Rasch shook off the enticing thoughts plaguing him, thoughts of the beguiling dark-haired woman with Gypsy bells. It was time they both got some sleep, time they severed the connection that became more forceful with every touch.

Rasch turned away from the fire and began to remove his clothes until he got down to his underwear and socks. He shoved them inside, then crawled into the small tent and into his sleeping bag. He didn't have to look to know that Savannah had watched his every move. The burning sensation at the base of his skull said that she had. Long after he'd closed his eyes, the heat of her gaze still burned his skin.

Four

The fire died down. The water in Shadow Lake spilled over its dam and rippled away down the mountain. The sounds of the night creatures gradually filtered through the silence, timidly at first, then more boldly as they went about their routine.

Rasch felt relaxed. He felt good. Though he wondered about his companion, why she had sought him out and what her true intentions were, he fell asleep with surprising ease. It was much later when the peppering of raindrops on his tent awakened him. He opened his eyes, startled for a moment before he became oriented. It was raining.

Savannah! Rasch unzipped his bag and crawled to the front of his tent. By the sizzling embers of the fire he could see a hunched-up mass. She was sitting up, covered with her bedroll. So much for the good-weather forecast.

"Come inside, Gypsy. I don't want you to drown."

"I'll be all right," Savannah managed to say between chattering teeth.

"You won't be all right. Believe me, I've camped up here before. From the sound of this, it isn't going to stop anytime soon. I promise you, there's enough room in here for two."

Savannah wanted to argue, but she was too miserable to do it. Just because they shared a tent didn't mean they had to share the same bag, she reasoned as she stood up and began to drag her cover with her.

"Leave your bag outside, it's wet."

"But—"

A crack of lightning split the sky, and Savannah felt as if a garden hose were pouring water all over her. If the bag hadn't been wet before, it was now. Thunder rolled down the mountain across the lake and ended in another flash of lightning over her head. She dropped the bag and scrambled into the tent, her knees on the warm inner lining of Rasch's sleeping bag.

Shivering, she crawled forward and slid as far into the bag, away from Rasch, as she could get. Still, when he lay back down, he was swamped with her damp skirt and petticoat.

"Sorry, Savannah, but those wet clothes have to go. I can't even close the bag. It's me or your skirts, and this is my bag. Take them off."

"But surely you don't expect me to sleep in here with you—without clothes?"

"Why not? People have been doing it for centuries."

"But—but, I didn't plan on—at least not yet. *Oh!*"

Rasch almost chuckled when he heard what she'd said. Twice, under pressure, she'd given away details she hadn't intended to. First that it had been she on his balcony and now that she had planned on sleeping with him—not now, but at some future date. He almost smiled, until he realized that she was trying to slide the skirt and petticoat off without getting out of the bag, and without touching him. But it was a futile attempt.

"Here, let me help." He reached under the bag and caught the waistband of her skirt. His fingers touched the soft inner flesh of her abdomen, and he felt her silent gasp. She was half frozen. With a quick motion he jerked the wet garments down and away from her feet, pitching them out of the tent.

"Now the blouse."

"No. I mean, it isn't too wet."

"Maybe not, but it's damp, and I don't want the inside of this bag to get wet. Our bodies will keep us warm."

"I just bet they will," she said, anger beginning to override her chill.

Rasch disregarded her fury, and pulled the blouse over her head. It followed the skirt out of the tent. Then he drew Savannah back to the mat, sliding his long frame back inside, and began to fasten the bag.

He'd been wrong about the skirt. Even with it gone, the bag still fought his efforts to zip it. It was a large bag, big enough for two, he'd thought, but it was obvious that the two people had to be very well acquainted.

"Sorry about this, Gypsy, but we're going to have to get closer, or this thing isn't going to reach."

Savannah felt him inch nearer. She was lying on her side, ramrod-straight, her arms crossed over her breasts, trying desperately to keep her very breathing from forcing them to touch. By the time he'd zipped

the bag completely, it didn't matter; they were together, shoulder to thigh.

"You're frozen," Rasch said as he turned on his
side, drawing her back against his chest. He slipped
both his arms around her so that her head was
resting on one arm while he curved the other around
her shoulder.

"What are you doing?"

"I'm going to get you warm."

"I'm warm enough."

"For an Eskimo, maybe. I don't look forward to
having a sniffling, bleary-eyed companion on this
hike, which is just what's going to happen if you
catch a cold on our first night out."

"I don't catch colds."

"And I don't take my responsibilities lightly. I don't
know what you had in mind for this little venture,
but if seducing me was part of the plan, this is your
chance. If not, then let me warm you up so we can
both get some sleep."

Savannah opened her mouth to protest, but the
delicious sensation that flooded her body when he
pulled her closer silenced her. He threw his leg across
hers and began to massage her feet with his feet, her
arm with his arm, and her face with his fingertips.
The electric shock of his flesh against hers took away
all thought of speech.

Instead, she felt her traitorous body begin to respond, becoming aware of nerve endings returning
to life with a shivery sensation that danced along her
body like heat from a midday summer sun. Her face
and neck tingled. She became aware of the hair on
his legs brushing against her, of his left hand working its way across her rib cage. Delicious sensations

surged through her, and she felt a primal yearning deep within her womanly recesses.

This time it was Rasch who took a quick, shallow breath. "You aren't wearing anything beneath that blouse."

"And you consider yourself a keen observer of people." She was finding it hard to breathe. "I thought you knew."

Rasch was having breathing problems of his own, and that was minor compared with the other reactions of his body. "I didn't. Ah, Savannah, it seems that I'm not as much in control as I thought. In lieu of taking a cold shower, maybe I'll go out and check the fire."

"Don't worry about the fire on my account," Savannah said softly. "I'm getting warm, very warm."

"So am I, Gypsy. Now close your eyes and go to sleep."

"All right," she agreed, feigning a yawn as she snuggled into the warm cocoon of his body. And then she felt his manhood, throbbing insistently against her bottom.

So, the crusader's body wanted hers. Good, that was a beginning. Thwarted passion was definitely a plus. He wanted to keep her warm. He was strung out with tension and eroding control. Good. She'd follow orders. She'd go to sleep and let him struggle with his honor; he certainly never had in court.

Blatantly Savannah wiggled her derriere, pressing it against the evidence of his desire. "I think you're right, Crusader," she said drowsily. "We ought to get some sleep."

For the next half hour they lay, each held in check, waiting for some evidence that the other was sleeping. But it wasn't happening. Every second was fuel for the smoldering embers of desire, until finally Rasch gave a loud groan and turned her over.

"You aren't asleep, and I can't sleep either. We've got to do something about this, or neither one of us will be worth killing in the morning."

His lips captured hers with unexpected abandon. For a moment she responded then his last words echoed in her consciousness. *Neither one of us will be worth killing in the morning.* Worth killing! For a moment she'd forgotten what she'd set out to do.

Letting Judge Horatio Webber make love to her might well be part of the outcome, but not when she was as emotionally overwrought as he—not yet. She had to make certain that the attachment was more than purely sexual if she was going to punish him for her brother's death. She wasn't about to let him make love to her before the time was right.

Savannah shuddered and pulled away. "Sorry, Crusader, I'm not interested in some fling in the hay, or bag, as the case may be. I seem to be warm enough, and come morning you'll be over this problem you have."

This time she finally managed to sleep. Whether it was the reminder of Tifton's death that made her renew her pledge to avenge her brother, or sheer willpower, didn't matter. All that mattered was that she slept.

And eventually Rasch slept too. When he woke the next morning, his hand was cupping her breast possessively. In the pale morning light he could see her face, relaxed now in sleep. She was smiling slightly and moving ever so gently beneath his hand. He could tell that her breasts were full, her nipples generous buds, her body taut and well-muscled. No wasted flesh on this lady. No fear or pushing away this time.

For a long moment Rasch let himself explore the softness of her skin, smell the elusive scent she'd identified as that of the tea olive blossom. He recognized the faintly permissive movements of her body pressing against his. She'd been wrong about the morning. He had no more self-control now than he'd had last night. If he didn't get up and out, he was going to do something foolish like roll over on top of her and bury himself deep inside that responsive womanly body.

He reached up and unzipped the bag, slipping away from the warmth of her flesh and being hit by the crisp, cool mountain air that followed a night of rain. He left the tent, carrying his clothes in his hands.

Savannah groaned in protest, until she came awake and realized what she was doing. From the open flap of the tent she watched Rasch stretch in the morning sun. His body was spectacular—lean, strong, and masculine. There were scars on his back, old scars, and she wondered what had happened to him.

He stared out into the early morning mist, a frown marring his handsome face, as if he were trying to make some decision that was distasteful. Then he pulled on his pants and a faded Harvard sweatshirt and moved out of her vision. For a few minutes she could hear him as he stirred the fire, then there was silence.

Savannah stretched. Her body still felt warm—and more. After a night of sleeping in the crusader's arms, she felt a banked heat simmering inside her. She contracted her muscles and felt a ripple of desire between her legs. Even in sleep their bodies had continued the connection. She was jolted by the knowledge that she wanted the crusader to make love to her. More than that, she needed it badly. And she wondered how she would get through the day without giving herself away.

Beyond the campsite, in the shadow of the trees, Rasch forced himself to take a long, deep breath as he tried to relax. He felt her on his skin, smelled her even now, and he was so strung out that he couldn't seem to slow his pulse. For most—hell for all—of the night as far as he could tell, he'd stayed hard, and that wasn't changing.

"Damn!"

A chipmunk sat on a log watching him will his body to cooperate. The small animal tilted his little masked face and waited for a minute before cocking his ears and beginning to chatter in intense animation.

Rasch didn't talk chipmunk, but eventually he recognized the message of alarm and turned back to their camp. Gypsy had been right; there were more things in heaven and earth than he'd ever dreamed of. And one of them was back in the tent, waiting for him.

The sound of bells filtered through his thoughts.

He began to peel off his shirt.

He knew what he was doing was insane. He'd never before done anything that wasn't carefully thought out and studied. But this morning Judge Horatio Webber didn't care to deliberate. He only knew that he wanted this woman, whoever she was, whatever her own agenda.

Rasch was halfway back to the campsite when he saw it—a very large black bear at the water's edge. Rasch came to an abrupt stop. "Oh, God!"

He'd joked about the danger of bears, but he'd never expected his warning to become a reality. Quickly he tried to formulate a plan. Nothing came to mind until he saw the bear swing around toward the fire, turning its head slowly back and forth as if puzzled or listening. The flap of the tent pushed open as Savannah crawled out.

"No!" Rasch flung off his unlaced boots and broke into a run. "Savannah, don't move!"

The bear let out a threatening growl and jerked his attention away from Savannah and toward Rasch, who was waving his arms and yelling loudly.

Savannah felt her blood plummet to her bare feet as she realized what was happening. Not five feet away was an enormous bear, standing upright like a human and swaying back and forth in confusion.

On the other side of the fire the big, crazy man was trying to taunt the bear into coming after him. He was trying to save her life by drawing the animal's attack. Around the edge of the lake she saw a cub loping merrily toward the judge. The bear cub's mother was going to tear Savannah's crusader apart. There'd been a time she'd almost wanted him dead—but not like this.

"No!" Savannah tried focusing her concentration on the bear. She'd done it a hundred times at the circus, calming the excited animals when no one else could.

But this bear was too excited to respond to Savannah's telepathic message. The cub! Savannah turned her attention to the baby bear. With every ounce of her being Savannah channeled her mental impulses on the cub. *Stop! Go away! Go away!*

Just as the mother bear came down on all fours to give chase to Rasch, the cub squealed and turned, heading around the lake in the opposite direction. While Savannah's message to the mother met with a wall of resistance, the cub's cry cut directly through the confusion. The large bear came to a swaying stop, unable to decide whether to take vengeance on the man or see to her baby. Another cry from the cub settled the question, and the mother bear changed course and lumbered after her frightened offspring.

Following the bear's example, Rasch turned and jogged back to where Savannah was standing, white-faced and trembling.

"Are you all right, Gypsy?"

He gathered Savannah in his arms and held her, his heart pounding in unison with hers.

"Crusader, you idiot! Who do you think you are, Superman? That bear could have ripped you limb from limb! What did you plan to do, outrun it?"

"I don't know," he admitted. She was upbraiding him just as his mother had decades earlier, when he'd rushed into the street to jerk a smaller child out of the path of a speeding car. His mother had been afraid too. Now Savannah's arms were holding him, clinging to him desperately. She made no attempt to hide her fear.

"Suppose you'd been killed? I need you." She wasn't making any sense. Fear had loosened her tongue. Not fear for herself, but for Rasch. "Oh, Crusader . . ."

This time they initiated the kiss mutually, lips merging, tongues plundering simultaneously, bodies pressing into each other as if fused. Her arms twined around his neck, drawing his head down and holding him as tightly as he was holding her.

His tongue withdrew momentarily to circle her lips possessively as if branding them his, then reentered her mouth to parry and thrust as his hands found the voluptuous globes of her breasts and fondled them lovingly, masterfully.

He didn't speak. He couldn't. All he knew was that he'd almost lost her before they'd given free rein to the passion that flamed between them. There was no holding back now, no resistance, no reluctance.

They were inside the tent again, leaving their clothes on the damp grass outside as they explored each other's bodies with wonderment and yearning.

With expert hands he stroked her breasts, rolling the nipples between his fingers until she cried out with delicious agony. Leaving a trail of butterfly kisses down her neck and shoulder, he captured one hard bud in his mouth and began to lave tantalizingly with his tongue, while his hand found her womanly wetness and played sweet music there until she thought she'd swoon. She reached for him then, feeling in his swollen manhood all the molten desire that coursed through her, and as he lifted himself above her, lightning sparks seemed to explode wherever heated skin touched heated skin.

Savannah forgot her plan, forgot to exult in her success as they joined in the ultimate intimacy and became one flesh, one being. They'd escaped death, and that was all that mattered. He'd risked his life for her, and each thrust of himself in her welcoming sheath brought her new life, new rapture.

She wanted him, Rasch thought crazily, as much as he wanted her. They were irrevocably connected now, soaring with the gods. Olympus was reached and surpassed when their release flung them into a corner of the heavens before sending them floating back to earth in a dreamy state of tranquillity.

He lay suspended in the wonder of the moment before he felt the brisk air slap his bare backside. With a groan of regret he rolled to his side, drawing Savannah into his arms, bringing the sleeping bag over them as an intimate cocoon.

Making love with this Gypsy woman was so incredible that he couldn't begin to believe what he'd experienced. This was some waking dream, some erotic fantasy he'd conjured up. He closed his eyes, determined not to think or question. He just wanted to feel.

Rasch cared about her, really cared. The idea broke over Savannah like the icy wind from which Rasch had tried to protect her. She was lying in his arms, still caught up in the ecstatic satiety of their lovemaking, still tingling from the wonder of the feelings he'd evoked. She never expected to experience such rapture, such fulfillment. Even now she could barely believe what had happened.

For weeks she'd plotted her revenge. She'd make the judge fall in love with her, make him want her beyond reason, then she'd disappear, leaving him hurting just as she and her father had hurt when Tifton had died. At one point she'd actually considered killing the man who'd just risked his life to save her.

But the conflicting emotions raging through her were being overwhelmed by a stream of euphoria, delightful feelings of being cherished and exalted. She couldn't close them off. Rasch cared about her. Her plan seemed to be working, she decided as she felt the renewed movement of his fingertips on her breast. Or was it only that she was caught up in a web of her own spinning?

At the moment she couldn't seem to think clearly. All she could focus on was the knowledge that she'd have to leave soon. But, she rationalized, the miracle of their single joining was enough for her. She couldn't be sure about Rasch, though. She wouldn't leave yet—not until she was certain of the outcome. Making love to Rasch had been the undefined part of her plan; enjoying it was simply an unexpected benefit, she told herself as she slid her leg across his thighs and pressed against him.

"You risked your life for me," she whispered. "How did you know the bear was there?"

"I didn't. It was the chipmunk," he answered, burying one hand in her hair while the other encircled her breast.

"The chipmunk?" He was suffering from aftershock, or maybe it was her. She was again falling under the spell of his lips and the tantalizing sensations aroused by his caresses.

"I went into the woods to take a—to, well, anyway, while I was there, a chipmunk jumped up on a log. I thought he was just laughing until I realized that he was trying to tell me something, something urgent."

"A chipmunk told you that I was in danger?"

"Yes. I don't know how, but I knew."

Savannah was stunned. Outside of a few people in

the circus, she'd never known of anyone besides herself to have that kind of link with animals. She never expected Rasch to acquire it. "It isn't hard to communicate," she said softly.

"Yesterday I wouldn't have believed any of this, Gypsy, but you seem to have some strange power over my mind as well as my body."

"Your body?"

"Yes. It's communicating its needs quite distinctly. Can you feel it?"

"Oh, yes," she said.

This time their ascent to the heavens was slow and delicious. And he was right. There was a power in their lovemaking. Power and release. Gentleness and warmth. Savannah fell asleep in her lover's arms. It wasn't until later, when she waked happy and content, that she faced the truth. Her plan had been altered.

Outside the tent the sky had cleared and the sun made little diamonds of light on the water. Rasch was whistling. She heard him before she crawled out of the tent and searched the area, finding him standing beside the water holding a handmade fishing pole.

At the sound of her movement he turned around and smiled. "As much as I like you that way, Gypsy, you'd better put on your jeans and shirt. It's pretty nippy out here."

Savannah could have tried to cover her nudity as she retrieved her pillowcase, but it seemed a bit late for modesty. Besides, she liked the idea of him staring at her body, responding to her as she knew he was. The magnetism was as strong between them now as it had been in the truck when he'd first invited her to get in. Almost reluctantly she pulled on underwear and her new clothes. She sat and donned her red socks and boots, feeling the heat of his gaze with every move she made.

Her plan was definitely working—perhaps too well. There was a danger in that. It was Rasch alone she wanted to fall in love, Rasch alone who was supposed to become besotted, not her.

Something tightened in her throat. Fear? Desire? She didn't know how to deal with that kind of emotion. She'd never been tested like this before. She had to slow things down, put some distance between them.

"About what happened, Crusader, I think we ought to talk about it," Savannah said hesitantly.

"What about what happened?" Rasch asked warily.

"It's understandable. I—I was afraid. We were caught up in the emotion of the situation, that's all. I don't think we ought to let it happen again."

That was the last thing he'd expected to hear. "I disagree," he said honestly. "Of course I know we were caught up in the fear of the moment, but personally I thought our lovemaking was"—his voice dropped lower—"was spectacular."

"Please, Crusader. I should never have yielded. I'm wrong for you. I'm a temporary kind of woman. And I think that you're a very permanent man."

"I thought you were a Gypsy, Savannah. A Gypsy doesn't question fate. How can you know who belongs together and who doesn't?"

"I don't know, Crusader. I'm just a simple voyager, a traveler, sharing your trail for a while. I don't have any answers. But I think we need some time, some distance . . ."

Rasch looked at her, noting the confusion in her

eyes, the way she folded her arms across her body and hugged herself, as if she were trying to hold back the natural feelings that they'd shared. He didn't understand her reluctance or the distance she was putting between them after this morning, but he couldn't force himself on her.

Making love had to be her choice, made freely. For now he'd wait. There was still much he would learn about his mystery woman, and learn he would, sooner or later. They still had nine days, and he didn't believe for a minute that she could stay out of his arms.

"Have you caught anything?" she finally asked, trying to curtail her response to his signals as she came to stand beside him.

"Our breakfast, or, rather, considering the time, our lunch." He took a deep breath and stepped away. Giving her time was very hard to do when she was so close.

"I'm sorry, am I disturbing you?"

"Hell yes. You disturb me continuously. You turn me inside out just by standing there."

"I'm sorry. I'll go back to the fire."

"No. Stay. It isn't your fault that all I want to do is kiss you to smithereens and feel you against me."

"Yes, it is," she answered honestly. "But you have a quest, and so do I."

"At this moment, Gypsy, I think I could cheerfully spend the rest of my life right here on this riverbank. But unfortunately I have to be in Asheville in nine days. I restarted the fire. Why don't you check on it while I clean the fish."

But the lightness had gone out of the day. Savannah didn't want to think about leaving. She didn't want to think about what she'd lose by refusing to continue what they'd shared. She hadn't planned on the bear. And she was still struggling with her reaction to their lovemaking. She needed some time to think and perhaps reformulate her plan. For now, all she could do was try to conceal from him her true feelings.

"Do you think our bear left?" she asked brightly.

"According to the birds, she did."

Savannah looked up, startled to find that he'd moved back beside her. "You're communicating with the birds now too?"

"Communicating? Yes, I think so. I feel as if my body is in tune with the universe. You did that to me."

"I did?"

He frowned, gave her a quick, hard kiss, and let her go. "Yes. I don't know why you're having second thoughts. No matter what you say, you've cast a spell over me, my Gypsy queen. You've changed my life forever."

A cloud passed briefly over the sun and cast a shadow on Rasch's face. Savannah shivered. "No, no spells, I haven't put my spell on you, not yet."

What he'd said was too close to the truth. She'd intended to fascinate him, mystify him, make him intensely aware of her. She'd never paid much attention to Zeena's claim that Gypsies had certain powers to seduce and claim a man's soul. Not until she'd determined to capture the judge. Still, she hadn't tried any of the incantations she'd learned. The bag of love potions Zeena had pressed into her hand was still unopened in her bag.

Quickly Savannah added wood and poked at the

fire. Her skirt and blouse had been rinsed in the lake and were draped across the grass beside her sleeping bag to dry in the sun. Consciously she averted her eyes away from Rasch as she walked past him to fill the coffeepot from the lake. Using green sticks cut from a willow beside the lake, Rasch threaded them through their fish, fashioning a rotisserie, and set them to roast over the fire.

The smell of the cooking fish filled the air, and Savannah realized how hungry she was.

They broke off hot chunks of the fish and blew on them to cool them before filling their mouths. Between the two of them, they ate all four fish Rasch had caught, washing them down with the hot coffee.

"Tell me about yourself, Gypsy," Rasch said, licking a sliver of fish from his fingers. "Where do you live when you aren't dropping from the sky or disappearing in a puff of smoke?"

"I live everywhere and nowhere," she said vaguely.

"Sure, and you charm strangers into buying you food and clothes, and providing you with transportation?"

"No. Not usually. I travel with friends. You know us Gypsies. We take care of ourselves."

Rasch leaned back on his elbows and stared at her. "How?"

The conversation was becoming too personal. Her best hope at evasion was to continue the Gypsy fantasy he'd latched on to. "Off the land and our skills," she said playfully, standing. "Right now I'm going to wash these things and pack our supplies."

As she leaned over, gathering up the remains of their meal, her breasts pushed against the fabric of her shirt. The jeans, tight and new, hugged her lush curves. He heard the light tinkle of her bells as she rinsed the dishes in the lake. She might have removed her Gypsy clothing, but the bells were like her fragrance, a subtle reminder of her voluptuous mystery. Leaving the water's edge, she sat down to braid her hair into a long plait that hung down her back.

Her hair, uncombed and wildly tousled a moment ago, made Rasch remember his earlier thoughts of how she'd look rolling from a man's bed. A man's bed? *His* bed. His pulse began to race. Had it been only twenty-four hours ago?

"Where will we camp tonight?" she called out.

The thought of what the night would bring made it hard for Rasch to concentrate on an answer to her question. He was practically in thrall to the woman and the spell she was weaving around him. When Jake had told him to find a woman and try to relax, Jake never knew what he was suggesting.

"It depends on how fast we move."

Rasch felt a stirring in his body, an eagerness that was new and exciting. The chattering of an overhead bird seemed an admonition to forget about questions and answers. He watched as Savannah put the final twists in her braid and fastened it with a ribbon. She was so beautiful, so wild, so enchanting. He felt as if he'd stumbled into Brigadoon, and that if he closed his eyes, it would disappear. She had to have been as surprised as he over the intensity of their lovemaking. For her as well as for himself, the pleasuring had to have been beyond anything previously experienced, and in the emotional domain as well. That was why she was backing away. He wouldn't think about tonight. He'd wait until she was ready to love him again. In his heart, he knew she would be.

Suddenly all the worry and indecision he carried around with him vanished. The courtroom seemed a thousand miles away. Crime, misery, pain—all gone. He had nine days before he had to face reality again.

Rasch began to whistle as he took down the tent and folded it. He shook out the sleeping bag, breathing in the lush, sweet smell of the tea olive blossoms, her smell, the fragrance that he'd carry with him always. In no time they were moving again.

She'd been the one to pull away. He hadn't been strong enough to do it.

She wanted time. That was probably wise. Fine— they'd be two people traveling together, nothing more. For now there would be no more questions.

But even as he censored himself, he knew that the truth was somewhere in the distance, waiting, yet submerged in the physical awareness of two people who touched without touching and connected with each touch.

They had nine more days.

He could wait.

Five

Rasch and Savannah made camp by a waterfall the following night, sleeping apart in silent misery. Each waited for the other to reach out. Neither did.

Daytime was better. For the next two days they climbed steadily, pausing now and then to enjoy a spectacular view of a valley or a mountain in the distance.

Savannah stayed close, not appearing to be winded or tired. As she'd said, the new boots didn't bother her. Neither did the physical exertion. She seemed to thrive on the exercise, letting her laughter come free and easy as they exchanged information.

Rasch was beginning to see to what extent Savannah was an exceptional woman. She didn't need conversation or reassurance. She knew how to enjoy the quiet beauty of the woods. She found wildflowers still blooming in protected spots. Wild animals didn't hesitate to show themselves when they stopped to view a special tree or scene. There was an innocence about her that made the day brighter.

Rasch felt as if he were traveling through a fantasy land surrounded by the animals who were always there, just out of sight, but a part of their caravan. And he sensed that Savannah was touched by what was happening as well. She constantly reached back to take his hand and point something out to him. Each time she held it a little longer and released it more reluctantly.

Rasch shed his brusque demeanor, and Savannah liked the gentle, vulnerable man who emerged. He talked about his childhood and his mother, who'd tried so hard to defeat the demons that possessed her. About how he'd decided early on that he would never endanger anyone he loved by bringing them into the kind of life where they might be threatened by the world's evil. There was no time for personal commitments. He'd directed his energies to reach his goal.

Savannah could understand that. Even as a child she'd understood commitment. And she'd focused on taking her mother's place, caring for her father and her brother. Her goals had been less grand than Rasch's, but no less important. The circus became her world, and that world had closed out personal relationships too.

The hours passed too quickly. When there was a log to be climbed over, Savannah readily accepted Rasch's help. They were working their way back to intimacy, but they weren't there yet. Still, each was content to wait.

Midafternoon of the third day they reached Walasy-Yi Center at the base of Blood Mountain. The center offered a little store where campers could send and pick up mail or make telephone calls. While Rasch was signing the campers' registry and buying more supplies, Savannah pushed aside her growing reluctance to call Niko and forced herself to find a pay phone.

Given the intense sexual tension between them, she'd decided that six more days with the judge might be a mistake—not for the judge, but for her. She'd caught Rasch in her web of desire. But she'd snared herself as well. Savannah knew that she'd have to bring their intimacy to an end while she could still leave.

Niko was confused when she couldn't explain her reason for cutting short the hike. Savannah wasn't sure she understood herself. She just knew that she was finding it harder and harder to keep herself out of Rasch Webber's arms. Directing Niko to drive to the center and wait for further instructions, she hung up the phone.

"Who were you talking to?" Rasch asked casually as he exited the store at the same time Savannah left the phone booth.

"Just checking in with my friends, to make sure they're all right," she answered too quickly to sound casual.

"And are they?"

"Ah, yes, there was a—a mix-up about our meeting. It was to be next weekend instead of this one." She covered her lie with a question. "Tell me about Blood Mountain. How did it get such an awful name?"

"It goes back to the Trail of Tears," Rasch began, relating the tale as they started out again. "General Winfield Scott was assigned to round up the Cherokees and move them west. Many refused to leave. Legend is that the battle they fought was so fierce that the streams ran red with blood."

Rasch took her hand as if to defend her. Savannah gave in to the warm feeling of protection that came so readily when she and Rasch were together.

As they ate their evening meal, the sexual tension between them was so strong it was palpable. Savannah went through the motions of eating but didn't taste the food. All their conversations died in mid-sentence until at last, tense and frustrated, they spent a sleepless night in silence.

The next morning brought warm sunshine. By late afternoon they'd made little progress up the trail. As if by mutual agreement, they'd let go of all restraint. One stop after another had brought them together, laughing over the antics of the animals, who seemed to fear them less and less, examining roots and herbs that could be used for ancient medicines, and simply talking about movies they'd seen and books they'd read.

Whether it was the growing ease of being close, or the knowledge that their relationship had taken a new direction, Rasch knew that they'd gone as far as they could without being together physically again. They were practically walking the trail arm and arm. Whatever doubts Savannah had about their lovemaking seemed to have vanished. Whoever his Gypsy was, she wanted him as much as he wanted her. He knew that, and she knew it too. Tonight they'd make love again.

Rasch called an early stop and moved off the trail to make camp in a clearing beside the ever-present mountain stream. After the rain of the first night the days had remained sunny and cloudless. Tonight, as they had for the last three nights, they'd sleep beneath the stars. Tonight they'd lie in each other's arms and—

Breaking off this line of thought, Rasch began giving Savannah instructions that she followed without question. They built a fire, banking it carefully so that they wouldn't cause a spark to escape. Savannah filled the pots and boiled the water while Rasch unpacked his sleeping bag and unfolded it. He picked up Savannah's, hesitated for a long minute, then retied it and laid it aside.

Savannah, watching out of the corner of her eye, gave a quick sigh of relief. For the last few days the tension had grown unbearably. It had been harder and harder not to slip out of her sleeping bag and crawl into his. Every touch, every shared moment, every smile, had fueled the fires that smoldered inside. She knew that tonight was the night to take the next step.

The crusader's action signified that he, too, was ready to end the separation. He wanted her. He intended them to sleep together again. Perhaps she should voice a protest. But Savannah knew by the pounding of her own heart that she wouldn't refuse. She didn't want to.

They poured dehydrated soup mix into the water and drank it from their coffee cups, sprinkling little bits of crackers into the liquid. Afterward, they rinsed the cups and filled them with cocoa mix and sipped the hot, sweet beverage in companionable silence.

"Are you tired?" Rasch asked eventually.

"No, not really. What I'd really like is a hot shower.

That's the one thing I miss, being on the road all the time."

"Oh?" Rasch didn't emphasize the question in his voice, choosing instead to take another sip of chocolate. He couldn't imagine an explanation for Savannah's inadvertent admission. *On the road?* She couldn't mean simply traveling, for anyplace she might stay, even the homeless shelters, had showers.

Homeless. Was that what she meant? If so, he could do something to help her. In his work with the courts and various charities, he knew the right people to contact. She'd mentioned a father, but that didn't mean he was still living.

"Don't you have any family?" he finally asked.

"Yes. I have a large family."

"Do they know where you are?" His question slipped out before he remembered his decision not to pry.

"Not precisely," she said, trying to keep her answers as honest as possible. She couldn't understand her sudden reluctance to lie. Perhaps it was tied in with his saving her life. More likely, it was because the less she strayed from the truth, the fewer lies she had to remember.

"Are you a runaway, Gypsy woman?"

Savannah laughed. "A runaway? Crusader, I'm twenty-seven years old, old enough to go where I like, when I like, do what I have to."

"No husband?"

"Oh." She hadn't considered that he'd think that. "No. I'm not married."

"I'm glad." And he was. He hadn't known how much the thought of a husband bothered him until he'd voiced the question. He didn't want Savannah to belong to another man. He wanted her to belong to him.

"How about you?" Savannah asked the obvious question. Though she knew the answer, he didn't know she knew, and she decided that she ought to respond as normally as possible.

Rasch laughed and stood up. "Me? Married? No. Would that bother you?"

Savannah drained the last of the chocolate from her cup. "Yes. I think it would. But I'm surprised. I should think that the proper wife would only enhance a judge's career."

"That's what Jake keeps telling me." Rasch began to collect up the dishes.

"Jake?"

"My friend. He's the mayor of Smyrna, a small town outside of Atlanta. He imagines himself as my campaign manager."

"Oh? Are you running for reelection?"

Rasch held out his hand to take Savannah's cup. "He has a notion that I'd make a good governor."

"And would you?" Savannah's heart began to pound. She hadn't intended to get caught up in Rasch's political career. She didn't want to know that he had dreams of public service.

"I don't know. I only know that there are serious problems in our state, problems that seem never to get the attention of those who make the decisions. I might have some ideas that would help make things right."

"And are you always right, Judge?"

"That's the second time you've asked that, Savannah."

He remembered. Savannah sprang to her feet. The

conversation was getting too serious. She opened her pillowcase and took out a cloth, her toothbrush, toothpaste, and a bar of soap.

"I may not have a hot shower, but I intend to take a bath, Crusader."

"Do you have any idea how cold that water is?"

"I've been cold and wet before," she answered, giving him a long look. "Why don't you build up the fire while I'm gone?"

Savannah sat down on a limb near the stream while she untied her boots and pulled off her socks, massaging her tired feet. Keeping an ear tuned to their campsite, she unbuttoned her shirt, took it off, and hung it on a bush. She unzipped her jeans and stepped out of them.

The woods were silent.

Giving a small prayer that there were no snakes lurking nearby, she stepped into the icy water. "Brrrrr!" Quickly she brushed her teeth and laid the brush and tube on the bank. Gritting her teeth in determination, she rinsed her socks and underwear, then began to soap herself. Just when she was certain she was half frozen, she heard a splash behind her and felt herself being caught in her crusader's arms.

"You're going to catch pneumonia or turn into an ice sculpture," he said in a voice that was hoarse with emotion. He tightened his arms around her and lifted her legs around his waist.

"Would that be so bad?"

"I'd probably come back here and sit in this stream until I was as frozen as you," he said. "Then we could melt together."

Their teeth chattered both from the cold and desire

as they rinsed the soap from their bodies. Rasch lifted her in his arms and strode back to the fire, blazing now in its circle of rocks. "Stand here," he said as he pulled a towel from his pack and began to dry her.

By the time they'd dried each other, they were warmed by the touch of hands and fabric, interspersed with kisses that heated their blood and fired their nerve endings with anticipation. When Rasch deposited Savannah on the sleeping bag, she didn't need the bag zipped to protect her from the cold. The North Georgia Mountains had become the Garden of Eden and they were man and woman at their most primitive and elemental.

"Unbraid your hair," he whispered. "I like you free and wild."

"Free and wild?" she repeated. "I wonder if anyone can be free and wild. . . ." She sat up and began to thread her fingertips through her plait, feathering her hair into a mass of luxuriant waves. The firelight reflected in the little beads of water still hanging in the dark hair. She looked as though she were wearing a crown of flames.

"You are free and wild, Gypsy. You're the most beautiful woman I've ever known."

"Only here, Crusader, in the wilderness. If we were back in the civilized world, there would be rules to follow and laws that would crush me."

There was a sadness in her voice that brought Rasch to a sitting position. He drew Savannah back to the mat and pulled the bag over them. "Never," he said. "I'd protect you—always."

Then he kissed her, and she returned his kiss in warmth and sadness. *No, my Crusader. You're the one I have to be protected from. Even you can't go back and do things over. You can never make things right for me. You've already hurt me too much.*

But she forgot her misgivings as he caught her up in the power of his touch. Perhaps there'd come a time when their lovemaking would be gentle and sweet, but now it seemed that each time they loved, their passion intensified. The heat was more searing, the ecstasy more extreme, the release more vivid.

"Savannah," he whispered, "I never expected to find anyone like you. You've filled a void in my life that I didn't know existed."

Lying in his arms, Savannah looked up at the night sky. The moment had come. She choked back panic and regret, trying to speak in a normal voice. "Horatio, you're quite a surprise to me too."

"Savannah, nobody has called me Horatio since my mother died. My friends call me Rasch. I'd hope that we're more than friends."

"Yes, Rasch is nice, but I like Horatio. Your mother was right. It sounds important," she said brightly— too brightly. "What happened to your mother?"

"She died with I was in college. I think she wanted to die. Her body gave out, and she was tired of struggling to be strong for me."

"I'm sorry," Savannah said quietly. "My mother died, too, when I was nine."

"How?"

"There was an accident. She fell. She was horribly injured, and I think that she willed herself to die. She didn't want us to see her like that."

Two mothers who chose to die, Savannah thought. *Two mothers who never knew each other,* and had nothing in common except one future moment that would bring their children together. She shivered. She didn't want to feel any emotional attachment to Judge Horatio Webber. She didn't want to think they had anything in common. She didn't want to begin to understand the man.

"There's the North Star, Horatio. Do you see it?"

Rasch turned his face to the heavens. "Yes, that's the bright one, isn't it?"

"Did you know that the North Star never moves? There's a legend about that."

The fire had died down to a mass of orange coals cracking comfortably in the silence. Rasch felt better than he had in a very long time. They'd shared danger and incredible lovemaking. They'd gotten to know each other, and they'd been joined in the ultimate communion. Now was the time for soft talk and being close. He adored hearing Savannah's husky voice. It mattered little what she said.

"Tell me the legend."

"There was once a Gypsy woman who fell in love with a god. He took her to the heavens to live. She could move back and forth between heaven and earth, and she could have anything she wanted, except for the fruit of one tree in his garden. If she ate of that fruit, the tree died, and its death left a hole in heaven. Time passed, and the Gypsy had a daughter. Her husband was happy beyond measure. The beautiful Gypsy was so loved and cherished that she grew spoiled. One day she was walking in her garden. She was hungry. She didn't believe that her husband would dare punish her, so she ate the fruit."

Savannah snuggled closer, as if she needed Rasch's protection. She felt the stubble of his beard against her cheek as he held her for a long moment. "What happened?"

"The tree died, and there was a tear in the fabric of heaven. The god was very disappointed. His beautiful Gypsy had to be punished; that was the rule. But he couldn't bear to harm her. Instead, he filled the space with her body. All the other stars continued to move about the heavens, but the Gypsy is destined forever to remain in one place so that the heavens are whole again."

Rasch moved his lips from her forehead to her cheeks. They were moist. She'd actually shed a tear for the beautiful Gypsy destined to be punished for her dishonor by remaining in one place forever.

"But look," he said, "she's the brightest star in the heavens, and she's the one by which we all find our way. So her plight wasn't all bad."

"Yes, that's true. Remember that, Crusader. Remember that about the fate of the Gypsy."

"If you're comparing yourself to her, don't. There are no forbidden trees along the trail. All their yields have been harvested by the animals to feed themselves for the winter."

Maybe, Savannah thought as she felt his lips move lower. *And maybe I've already tasted the forbidden fruit.*

The next morning when Rasch woke, Savannah was not in his arms. He came lazily to his feet and looked around. She was probably taking another icy bath in the stream. He pulled on his clothes and collected more wood to coax the fire back to life. The sun was shining. The temperature was cool, but the day would likely warm up. Rasch began to hum. He couldn't recall when he'd felt so happy.

Feeling his pulse quicken, he took the coffeepot he pushed through the undergrowth to the stream. Maybe an icy bath was a good way to start both their mornings.

But Savannah wasn't there. She wasn't anywhere around the campsite either. The bear! He tore through the brush, looking for signs of a struggle. There were none. Then, taking quiet stock of the situation, he realized that her backpack and camping gear were gone. There was nothing left in the camp to prove she'd ever been there.

Rasch sat down and tried to make sense of what had happened. She was gone. She'd left of her own accord. Quietly, stealthily, she'd slipped out of his arms, packed her supplies, and disappeared into the night. Only the lingering smell of tea olive blossoms kept him from believing that it had all been a dream.

His erotic fantasy was over.

His Gypsy was gone, and he didn't even know her full name.

The week after the conference Rasch was going through the motions, but nobody knew better than he that his heart was not in his job. His eyes constantly searched the courtroom, hoping that he'd see a laughing dark-eyed nymph in a Gypsy skirt. But she wasn't there. And there were no tingling nerve endings, no burning sensations on his neck that said he was being watched. At last he was forced to admit that she wasn't coming back.

"What's wrong, Rasch?" Jake asked, worry evident in his eyes. They were having dinner in a little restaurant on Peachtree. "You haven't been the same since I picked you up on the trail. What happened?"

"I met someone—a woman."

"So, what's the problem?"

"I—I don't know where she is."

Jake laid down his fork and widened his eyes. "What do you mean, you don't know where she is. Did you lose her someplace?"

"You could say that. We were hiking together. For four days we were—together. Then she was gone—just disappeared without a trace. I don't even know her name."

"Whoa! You spent four days camping with a woman and you don't know her name? What was she, a ghost?"

"Something like that." Rasch hesitated, rolling a piece of bread between his fingers until he'd sprinkled his pasta with the crumbs. "I guess I'd better tell you all of it. The first time I saw Gypsy, she appeared on my patio in a fog, at midnight."

"On your patio," Jake repeated, shaking his head. "Rasch, you live in a fourth-floor condo."

"I know, believe me, I know. It gets better. The second time was at Underground Atlanta, that night I climbed the flagpole to scan the crowd. Remember?"

"Oh, yes, the woman with the ribbons in her hair. So you found her. You don't have to keep her a secret, Rasch. You know that I've thought for some time you'd have a better chance at the governorship if you were married."

"You don't understand, Jake. The third time she appeared in the fog beside the road to Amicalola Falls. She was waiting for me."

"Waiting for you on the road? I don't think I like this, old buddy. Why?"

All pretense of eating was curtailed. The waiter took away the half-eaten plates of pasta and refilled their coffee cups before Jake motioned him away.

"I'm still not sure. Nothing happened—at least nothing I might have expected."

"But *something* happened, didn't it, old friend? She got to you somehow."

"I guess she did. Then I woke up one morning, and she was gone. I haven't been able to get her out of my mind. Every time I close my eyes, she's there—in court, in my bed, in my arms. I can't stop thinking about her."

"Great, here we are ready to start campaigning, and your mind is on some Gypsy girl. This, my friend, is not good."

Rasch lifted anguished eyes without trying to conceal his feelings from Jake. He'd gone over every word that was said, every moment of their time together, and he hadn't been able to come up with any answers. "I know."

"Okay, let's start with what little information we have. Why'd you call her Gypsy?"

"Because that's what she is. She travels around where there are no hot showers."

"So do truck drivers and cowboys." Jake shook his head. "What can I do to help?"

"Nothing, but thanks, Jake. I'll have to figure this out myself."

But another week passed, and Rasch was no closer to solving his mystery than he was the first day. The only thing he could think of was to go back to where he'd first seen her. Maybe the truck *had* been disabled. Maybe he could find the garage that repaired it.

He couldn't. There was no report of a breakdown. Rasch drove along the highway, replaying the conversation they'd had. He'd refused to see it, but it had been obvious from the beginning that she was waiting for him. She'd even admitted that she'd been on his balcony.

None of it made any sense.

By the time he reached the rangers' station at the falls, Rasch was beginning to see what he'd been too bemused to see before. And bemused was the right word. She'd appeared as a silver-haired spirit in the fog, wearing some kind of garment that made her look nude, knowing that he would be intrigued. Continuing to play on his fascination, she'd donned a red wig and shown herself in a smoky street, in a crowd where he couldn't get to her. And always she left behind the elusive scent of the tea olive blossom.

But why?

The more he tried to find logic in the situation, the more illogical it became. The only thing he was sure of was that Savannah had planned her assault well. She knew him . . . knew that he was burned out and lonely. She seemed to know instinctively that he needed someone. Judge Horatio Webber had allowed himself to be caught up in an erotic fantasy that had invaded his soul and wouldn't let go.

No, the forest ranger said, he hadn't seen Rasch's companion again, and nobody had inquired about her.

Rasch hastened to assure his friend Paul that he didn't think anything had happened to Savannah. She'd apparently just decided to go on without him, join her friends perhaps. Rasch covered his questions by saying that he simply wanted to make sure that she'd found them.

He realized that his explanation didn't satisfy Paul when the ranger pulled out the registry and began to study it. "Maybe some of these names will help." He ran his finger down the page. "Here you are, you and Ms. Ramey—"

"Ms. Ramey?" Rasch jerked the registry from Paul's hand and ran his fingers down the page. While Paul had been questioning Savannah about her plans, Rasch had signed in, giving his name, address, and destination. Beneath his name, in a bold flourish, was the signature of Savannah Ramey.

Apparently Paul had frightened her by saying that she shouldn't go alone. She hadn't wanted to run the risk of failure. She'd simply made ditto marks beneath Rasch's address and destination. But in the confusion she'd signed her name, Savannah Ramey.

Ramey. He finally had a name, a name that Rasch recognized all too well, a name that had been spread across the front page of the newspapers. Tifton Ramey, the young DUI he'd sentenced to jail, the boy who'd been killed by another prisoner.

All the way back to Atlanta, Rasch thought about Savannah and what had happened. Savannah and Tifton Ramey. The connection was established. He just needed the details. The next morning he fed the name into his computer, requesting a global search.

Within seconds he had the record before him.

Ramey, Tifton: twenty-one, charged with DUI, accident, and driving a stolen car. The jury found Tifton guilty, and Rasch had sentenced him to two years in jail.

A check of the court records revealed that the

address Tifton had given was phony. The police department was more helpful. It seemed that young Tifton Ramey had changed his mind about concealing his identity when he found out that the judge didn't intend to let him go. He'd sent for his sister, Savannah—Savannah Ramey, of the Ramey Circus, whose permanent address was a farm just south of Atlanta.

Callused hands and feet? Appearing and disappearing on balconies four floors in the air? Talking to animals? His Gypsy was a circus performer. And she'd stalked him. Why?

Rasch canceled his schedule for the rest of the day and headed south. The circus grounds were only thirty miles away. Thirty miles—Savannah was that close. He opened his windows and let the fall air clear his head as he practiced what he would say.

There was nothing he could do to bring her brother back. He didn't know how he could explain or justify his actions, except to be honest. Tifton was dead, and he was responsible. He regretted that she'd been hurt, but he couldn't change it. They just had to find a way to get through it and—

What? Resume their affair?

He was a superior court judge, and she was a Gypsy. What kind of relationship did he expect them to have? He thought about how they'd been together, how she'd felt beneath him, about the sound of her laughter and the smell of her perfume.

He didn't care. He'd find a way. Rasch glanced down at the speedometer and watched the needle climb. He just wanted to be with her—soon.

Six

Savannah stood outside her camper and stared at the sky. The North Star shone brightly, mocking her, reminding her that another Gypsy had once defied the man she loved and been punished for her actions.

With a sigh, she tried to erase the memory of the judge from her mind. Though angry when he'd learned what she'd done, her father seemed satisfied that she'd avenged her brother's death. Now he spent most of his time in his camper, letting Savannah and Niko look after the circus. Savannah didn't want to see the truth, but her father was growing old. He'd lost his fire.

Savannah seemed to have lost hers as well. Revenge wasn't supposed to be this way. The judge was to be the one who suffered—not her. She hadn't expected to miss him, or worry about what she'd done. But she did. She hadn't thought it would be so hard. She hadn't intended to care.

"What do you see up there, little one?"

Zeena stood beside her, and Savannah hadn't heard her approach.

"I wish I *were* little again. Life was so much simpler then, Zeena."

"Perhaps it still is."

"How can you say that, Zeena? Look around you. Our troupe grows smaller and smaller. Our animals are old, and our equipment is worn and needs replacing. And Father—all he does now is look at his newspaper clippings."

"It's very hard for your father. Everything he's ever done since he was a boy was for the future, his family's future. Now there is no longer a reason."

"What about me, Zeena? I'm a Ramey. This is my life and my heritage. How can he even think that there is no reason to go on?"

"Perhaps it's time for you to learn what you choose not to know."

"What do you mean, Zeena? Tell me what to do."

"I told you once—look beyond the anger and hurt and you will learn."

Savannah sighed. She was tired, so very tired. There was not enough money to carry them through the winter. The animal feed and veterinary bills were more than those to feed and care for the workers. Last week their animal handler announced that this would be his last year to work with the lions and tigers. They were already depending on newcomers for too much of the circus operation.

Through his window, Savannah could see her father. He was sitting in his favorite chair, staring vacantly at the scrapbook he was holding in his lap. Savannah knew what he was looking at. From the time she was old enough to be aware, she'd watched him cut out the newspaper clippings of his family. Beginning with her mother and father on the wires, continuing with Savannah and Tifton. But the book ended abruptly with Tifton's death.

Perhaps, Savannah thought, she'd made a mistake. Maybe she should have let her father seek revenge. Maybe if he'd done it himself, he'd be able to let go. Savannah felt as if she'd lost something special, and her loss had been for nothing.

"Crusader," she whispered, then wished she could call back the words. She'd tried not to say that name. As long as she thought about him as "the judge," it was easier not to want him. Now that she'd spoken his nickname, the memories were released, and they flowed over her like a blanket.

She remembered the sound of his laughter. His gentleness, the way his hands felt touching her breasts, kneading the pads of her bottom as he plunged into her. Her stomach muscles tightened, settling off a ripple of unexpected desire. Just thinking about him made her feel all liquid and breathless. One moment of memory brought her to the brink of ecstasy.

What was she to do? She couldn't go on like this!

Savannah took two steps toward her trailer, stopped, and turned away. Across the stubbled wheat field and into the trees she walked, listening to the sounds of the circus quiet down for the night. When she finally came to a stop, she was leaning against a low-growing branch of an oak tree, her head resting on folded arms.

And then she heard it, the silence. Not an animal

cried out. Not a leaf moved. The world was quiet. She sniffed and raised her head, glancing around.

"Who's there?"

A moan caught in her throat, a moan and a whimper. "Please? I don't like being teased."

"Neither do I, Gypsy."

The sound of his voice hit her like a whirlwind, beginning between her legs in a small vortex of heat that spiraled upward, compressing her chest and squeezing the breath from her lungs.

"Crusader?" The endearment escaped her before she could call it back. "Is that really you?"

"It's me." He could see her in the shadows as clearly as if the moon were shining on her. He'd watched her for hours, checking the camp, making her rounds, pacing back and forth inside her trailer, and finally seeking the freedom of the night.

"How did you find me?"

Rasch's emotions were whipping wildly back and forth. From the moment he'd caught sight of her examining the paw of one of the big cats, he'd wanted to lift her in his arms and carry her away from this place. But he hadn't been certain how she would react, so he'd waited until she'd left the confines of the camp and sought the privacy of the woods.

"Through Tifton."

She gasped. "Through Tifton? Are you trying to punish me, Crusader? How can you do this?"

He took a step closer. "I don't understand, Gypsy. I'm not trying to punish you. Punishment was *your* plan, I think. Why did you run away?"

"You think I could stay with you after what you did?"

"I don't know. At least we could have talked it out. After what we shared, you owed me that much."

Moonlight danced on Rasch's face and shoulders, turning his light hair into silver and his grave expression into sadness. He was a Michelangelo painting on a night sky, death and life, joy and sorrow.

Already the connection between them had begun, their auras touching in silent pleasure. The crisp air turned warm as the night came to life again. When Rasch reached out to take her hand, Savannah gave it. She could no more have stopped than she could have refused to breathe.

"You're right," she whispered tightly, "I should have told you the truth. I didn't know how. I'm sorry."

"No, I'm the one who's sorry, Gypsy. Sorry that I never contacted you or your father, sorry that an action taken in good faith had such hurtful consequences for you. What we had together was good, I won't accept any suggestion that it wasn't."

He couldn't take his eyes from her. She'd taken a step forward, out of the deepest shadows, and he could see the expression in her eyes. Anguish, disappointment, and yes, tears, were revealed in the velvet darkness beneath her lashes, the tears spilling over and making diamond chains across her face.

He thought back to the first times he'd seen her, on his balcony and in the street. She'd been sad then too. And that sadness had remained even after she disappeared. Every night when he closed his eyes, she'd be there staring at him censoriously. What did she think he'd done?

"You and I? That can't be, Crusader, not after what you did."

"I was never dishonest with you. I didn't disappear,

leaving you to wonder what you'd done wrong, leaving you to burn with wanting me, leaving you to die a little each day. Don't pretend that there is no connection between us."

Unable to hold back any longer, Rasch reached out and drew her into his arms, claiming her lips with a rough urgency that surprised even him. He could feel her whimper of panic turn into an acknowledgment of mutual need.

The kiss deepened. Crushing her lips, he felt her arch against him, taking his tongue inside her mouth as she pressed herself into his hardness. There was an oath, a moan, and their hands parted as his fingers slid shamelessly beneath her shirt, plying the soft flesh of her breasts, making the nipples grow taut and turgid with desire.

Tearing each other's clothes from their bodies, they fell to the pine straw, seeking fulfillment, solace for their pain. Rasch's deft hands sought the threshold of her desire, stimulating, teasing, beguiling her until she was mewing with desire.

"Say it, Gypsy, say you want me, that you want this as much as I do!"

"No, no, we mustn't."

Her words refused, but her body burned beneath his touch, and her lips tasted and bit at his mouth and chin as though she were lost and Rasch were her salvation.

"Listen, Gypsy, as I say the words. I want you. I want this tonight, tomorrow, and forever. Now you say it, Gypsy. Say it."

"All right! All right! I want you, and this. But I won't love you—I won't. I can't!"

Savannah groaned. She was sick with the realization of the truth of her words. She did want him. She wanted the feel of him inside her and enveloping her. A sweet, terrible pain swept through her as she parted her legs and felt him move to claim her body, touching, teasing, building the frenzy of heat that churned the very ground beneath them.

"Oh yes you will, my Gypsy, my wild and free Gypsy. I'll make you burn with loving me." He leaned back, then thrust into her with all the desperate longing he'd held back since she'd disappeared.

He didn't have to. She'd carried that same fire around inside ever since she'd left him. Now the fever inside them blazed into life, carrying them beyond reason, beyond caring, beyond restraint. And almost as quickly as they joined, they were caught up by such a vortex of rapture that Rasch thought he'd joined the realm of the superheroes of old. Stars burst, suns whirled through the heavens, and the tide of desire reversed, growing greater with each thrust instead of lessening with release.

When the final spasm of ecstasy sent vibrating fingers of fire through every cell, Rasch collapsed against Savannah, stunned and spent. For a long time he just lay across her, unsure whether this was real, or a dream. Then, drawing back, he looked into her eyes.

She lay there, equally stunned and confused. The fire was gone, the aftermath of their fever leaving them weak and shaking, waiting for him to speak.

"Are you satisfied, Crusader?"

"No," he answered, sliding from her body and rolling on his back. "I don't know what I am. I never intended anything like that to happen, Savannah. Believe me."

Savannah began to laugh, a low, whimpering sound that grew into a wild cry of disbelief. She came to her feet and began to run.

"What are you doing, Gypsy? Stop. What will your father say if you go back to the camp naked?"

Savannah came to a stop. "Oh, God, you've made me crazy. You expect me to forget that you're responsible for Tifton's death. Then you overpower me and make love to me."

"Wait a minute. I don't expect you to forget anything. I only want you to be fair."

Savannah turned and walked back to where Rasch was standing. She drew back her hand and would have slapped him with all the force she could manage if he hadn't seen the blow coming and grasped her wrist in midair. "I can't be—no matter what I want—I can't be."

As he continued to imprison her wrist, the color drained from Rasch's face, leaving him deadly white in the moonlight. His breathing stopped, and disbelief compressed his stomach muscles into a tight knot of pain.

"You don't know, do you, about your brother's trail of arrests across the entire Southeast? Nothing serious, not yet, but he was on the way. Only his charm had kept him out of jail before."

"You're lying, Crusader. My laughing, beautiful brother never hurt anybody in his life. He's dead, and you're responsible. Now my father is dying too."

Disbelief fell over Rasch like a blanket of ice. She didn't know about the petty theft, the speeding, the fights. All she knew was that he'd killed her brother. And he had. By sentencing him to jail, he'd made Tifton an example to the world that every man must accept responsibility for his actions. He could have let the young man off with a warning, but he hadn't, banking on a jail sentence showing him that drunk driving could kill.

It could.

It had.

Savannah's brother was dead, in a cell where he'd been sent by a judge full of his own importance and determination to do right.

Rasch turned loose Savannah's wrist and let her arm fall down beside her. He stared for a long time, absorbing the pain she felt, watching her sobs come to a stop and her tears dry up.

"So what were you going to do, Gypsy, kill me?"

"No, I wanted to hurt you like you hurt my father and me. I set out to make you fall in love with me. I wanted you to love something and lose it."

A wrenching pain began somewhere deep inside him and rose. He couldn't stop it. He couldn't control it. It overwhelmed him with the truth.

"You have, Gypsy. You've accomplished what you set out to do."

He turned and walked away, stopping to pick up his clothes, and disappearing into the darkness beneath the trees. She waited, trembling, so weak that a strong wind could have knocked her over.

Beyond the camp she heard an engine start and a vehicle drive away. She watched as long as the lights were visible, watched and felt her heart tear completely apart.

She'd made the judge fall in love with the Gypsy, and now she'd killed that love. Like the North Star, she'd be forever caught in the pain of her loss. An eye for an eye and a tooth for a tooth: the Gypsy way.

She'd settled her father's score, and she was the one who was dying.

The judge had fallen in love with the Gypsy, all right.

But the Gypsy hadn't meant to love him back.

Rasch drove slowly back to Atlanta, Savannah's accusation burning in his mind. Her brother was dead, tragically killed by a fellow inmate, and all he could do was tell her he was sorry.

Not only had he made Tifton an example, but he'd been proud of his righteousness. Sentencing prisoners, righting wrongs, being one of the upright, that was the goal he'd set for his life and he'd become an expert, swimming in the satisfaction of his success. He was Super Judge. Now he was ready to move on to the highest office in the state.

But he'd become a stiff-necked ass. He'd caused a young man's death with his self-righteousness. And it had cost him the only woman he'd ever cared about.

That night Rasch paced his apartment, onto the patio and back again, longing for the burning sensation that signaled Savannah's presence. But it didn't come.

He thought about the sad little circus with its patched tent, worn equipment, and peeling paint. He thought about Savannah and her father, and inside he cried.

"So she really is a Gypsy." Jake poured coffee into two cups and sat down at the kitchen table across from Rasch. Rasch had just stepped out of the shower when he'd arrived. He'd showered, pulled on a robe, and was drying his hair, an activity the old Rasch would never have done anywhere except the bathroom.

"Yes, a real Gypsy. Her grandfather brought his family to this country in the thirties. Circus life was all he knew, so he joined a small American troupe. Eventually he bought it, passing it along to Savannah's father. A few animals, a few kiddie rides and games of chance.

"For a man who didn't even know who his mystery woman was two weeks ago, you've learned a lot."

"Yes," Rasch said bitterly, "I've learned that I killed her brother."

"Damn! You killed somebody?"

"No, not directly, but I'm responsible."

"Tifton Ramey," Jake groaned. "The boy who died in jail. He was her brother?"

"Yes. Her name is Savannah Ramey, and now her circus is dying because of me."

"And you think that's your fault too?"

"No, it would have happened anyway. People don't need the circus anymore. With amusement parks and television, kids take a look at the Ramey show and want their money back."

"Then why are you beating yourself up? From what I can find out, this Tifton was no prize. If he hadn't been killed by another prisoner, it would have been something else."

"I went to see her, Jake. She holds me responsible. I have to do something. It doesn't matter how I feel about her."

"I get the idea that she wasn't too happy to see you. What happened?"

"Jake, I lost my head. Instead of telling her that I understood, I—we—well, I lost control."

"Did you hit her?" Jake couldn't keep the dismay from his voice.

"Hell no. We made love."

"Oh." Jake tapped his fingers on the table for a long minute. "You made love to her. But 'we' implies that the act was a mutual endeavor. So what's the problem?"

"I'm afraid that this incredible sexual desire between us is all there is, at least on Savannah's part. She hates me."

"And how do you feel? I mean other than the obvious."

"I like her. Can you believe that she was trying to set me up? She wanted me to fall for her, then she was going to hurt me like I hurt her father and her."

"And did you fall for her?"

"I think I did. She's beautiful, loyal, smart, and she talks to animals."

"Great! A governor's wife who communicates with animals. That could come in very handy."

"She'd never marry me, Jake. She's the kind of woman who has to be free and wild. I'd never try to change her."

"And you told her how you feel?"

"No, I never said the words. I might have, but she keeps running away."

"Interesting," Jake said, nodding his head. "I think I'll just check out this Gypsy, see for myself the woman who's turned Super Judge into a wimp."

"No, don't, Jake. I'll have to work this out for myself. I think I've been putting too many hours in on the job. I might just run away and join the circus."

"No, Rasch, what if the newspapers get wind of this? It could ruin your appeal as a candidate."

"You mean the voters wouldn't like a man who takes a menial job with a carnival?"

"I mean just that."

"Well, I think you're wrong. I think the people, the common man, would prefer someone who comes down from his ivory tower to learn the taxpayers' problems firsthand."

"Don't do this, Rasch. We need you on the bench."

"Oh, I don't intend to shirk my responsibilities. Judge Horatio Webber is going to moonlight, that's all." Rasch stood up, a broad smile curling his lips. "Thanks, Jake. I knew you'd have the answer."

"Look, Rasch," Jake began to argue. But Rasch wasn't listening. He had run away to join the circus. And to woo his Gypsy.

"So he's the one."

Savannah jumped. "Why do you keep sneaking up on me, Zeena?"

"I'm not sneaking up. I'm simply coming into the cook tent to have breakfast, as I do every morning."

"Zeena, you've never had coffee in this tent in your life before. You have your own coffeepot in your trailer."

"Today I felt like company, and a few answers. What are you going to do?"

"Do? I'm going to do what I do every day, see to the

operation of the Ramey Circus. I'm going to write letters about future bookings, open the mail, pay bills, and rehearse."

"Rehearse what?"

"On the wires, what else?"

"Oh, Savannah, can't you see what's happening?" Zeena sat down across from Savannah, settling her bulk into the folding chair gingerly. Everything about the circus was falling apart; the cook tent table and chairs were no exception.

"What's happening is what happens every fall—we settle in for the winter and plan next year's itinerary."

"And what month is this?"

"It's November."

"And when is fair season?"

"The fall, I guess." Savannah didn't want the conversation to go where Zeena was taking it. "At least it isn't cold yet. We don't have to worry about heating bills."

"Right, we don't. We have to worry about repair and maintenance bills, and we're doing it nearly a month earlier than we ought to. In years past we've been booked every week in November, sometimes even later. This year we aren't. Your father is tired, Savannah. He can't walk the wires anymore; he doesn't want to. He's ready to quit."

"It was all because of Tifton that he lost his drive. He'll get over that now. We'll find a way to hire some new acts, and by next spring we'll be ready to go again."

"No, Savannah, we won't. Sooner or later you're going to have to face the truth. The circus is finished. And it didn't have anything to do with Tifton. He would have left sooner or later. The only reason he stayed around for the time being was so he had a place to run to when he got in trouble."

"Zeena! How dare you? Tifton was—Tifton was good and kind and—"

"Tifton was wild and undisciplined, Savannah, and somebody always bailed him out. Your father loved him, and he tried to blame his death on someone else. But he knew. He never saw Tifton through rose-colored glasses like you did. Your brother was no innocent kid sowing his wild oats. The woman he hit wasn't killed, but she could have been. You've been wrong about Tifton. Maybe you're wrong about the judge too."

Savannah stared through the open tent, watching Niko as he washed down Nell, the last of their adult elephants. Beyond the compound was the big top. *Big top.* Even from where she was sitting, she could see the patches, patches that didn't quite keep out the rain when it was heavy.

Rain, falling on a tent. For a moment she was back in the tiny tent with Rasch. She straightened her shoulders, trying not to remember how protected she'd felt lying in his arms while he warmed her, trying not to acknowledge the instant desire that sparked between them or the frustration that stretched her emotions to the breaking point every moment they were apart.

Savannah focused on Tifton. She knew that Zeena was telling the truth about her brother. In the days since she'd been back, Savannah had been bombarded with conflicting emotions and memories. She remembered the first time Tifton walked the wire from one side to the other alone, how he grew more and more confident until, at fifteen, he was playing to the crowds with such charm that it became a game, figuring out which girl would be waiting behind the tent after the show. Then, as he grew older, he'd become reckless on the wire and off.

When had it changed? When had Tifton started drinking, fighting, driving too fast, taking such foolish chances? It was as if he weren't alive unless he was tempting fate. Had she been the last one to know?

Had she blamed her crusader for something that wasn't his fault?

Savannah turned back to answer Zeena and found she was alone. She hadn't heard the fortune-teller leave. In the distance she caught site of Zeena and her father, walking across the compound. They were talking. Her father was looking down at the fortune-teller with a smile on his face, the kind of smile his daughter rarely saw anymore.

Savannah went to the truck. She had to get away, to think. She'd had a call from a fellow circus owner who wanted to talk about a merger or an outright sale. This was as good a time as any to find out what he had to say. His company was playing just north of Atlanta for the week, far enough for a long drive and close enough for Savannah to be back by the next day. She stopped by the elephant lot and told Niko where she was going, and left instructions for the remaining crew members in camp.

Savannah drove slowly across the field to the highway, turning north. She opened all the windows and unplaited her braid, allowing her hair to fly in the wind.

That's the way the crusader liked her hair, free and wild, just as it was when they were together. She felt a tightness well up in her throat. What was she thinking of? A judge and a Gypsy? Only in legends and fairy tales. And Savannah was through believing in either.

Seven

Seven

Alfred Ramey was a tall man with tired dark eyes and a calm manner. He stood inside his trailer, just beyond the open door, studying Rasch.

"So you're the one who cursed our family. I've been waiting for you. Come in, Horatio Webber."

"How did you know?"

"I knew that you'd come sooner or later. I didn't know what you would say. I'm ready to listen."

Rasch put aside his reservations and stepped inside. An hour later he'd learned all he needed to know about the circus and Savannah, and he'd offered his proposition. Alfred Ramey didn't entirely believe that Rasch wanted to make restitution for the damage he'd done to the Ramey family, but he was too wise to refuse the opportunity to the man who held the key to his daughter's happiness.

"All right, Rasch," Alfred finally agreed. "But you need to know that this isn't really Savannah's fault. I closed my eyes to Tifton's faults just as she did. His death seemed to be an omen. I blamed you rather than accept losing our way of life."

"But I was responsible, Alfred. If I hadn't made an example of your son, he wouldn't be dead."

"We can't know what the Fates have in store for us, Rasch. If I hadn't been so angry, I would have stopped Savannah when she told me what she was going to do. I even approved. But I was wrong, and I don't want to lose her. What about you, Rasch—why are you here?"

"I don't know exactly. To try and make amends somehow to Savannah. I never meant to harm Tifton, just to teach him a lesson. I thought that he was heading for big trouble."

"I know. No matter how much I wish it were different, I've come to understand that Tifton was responsible for his own fate. And that same thinking tells me that Savannah is responsible for hers. I won't refuse your help, but I won't allow you to stay if she doesn't want you here."

"Fair enough," Rasch said with growing confidence. "What shall I do first?"

By the time Savannah returned the next morning, her trailer was wearing a new coat of paint, and Zeena's sign was bright red instead of a faded pink.

"Savannah? You're just in time," Niko called out, "we have a little job for tomorrow."

"What kind of job?" Savannah was tired and depressed. A new coat of paint on her trailer was a waste. The offer she'd got for their circus was so low that she'd laughed. The circus could never go another season without money, but she wouldn't give it away either. Still, unless she came up with a miracle, the circus might even have to close. Somebody meant well, but a little paint wasn't going to help.

"We've got two days at a children's home in East Point."

"A children's home? Niko, we can't afford charity."

"This isn't for charity. It's a money-making event, and we get part of the proceeds."

"It'll cost us more to set up than we'll make. Besides, we don't have enough help. There's nobody to leave behind to look after things here."

"Yes, there is, Savannah, we have a new hand."

"A new hand? Who? Where did he come from?"

"Your father hired him yesterday while you were gone. He's over in the animal compound washing out the cats' cages and cleaning up behind the elephants."

Her father had hired a new hand yesterday, knowing the state of their finances? It had been so long since he'd taken an interest in managing the circus. Savannah shook off the curious feeling of unease that was sweeping over her. The back of her neck began to prickle, and she felt slightly light-headed. Granted, she hadn't stopped to eat on the drive back, but this sensation was more than that.

Savannah was beginning to have bad vibes. She started to run.

He wasn't wearing a shirt. The scars on his back rippled as he leaned over to the shovel away from the refuse. A sheen of perspiration covered his well-muscled upper arms and chest, and his hair was tousled golden in the fall sunlight. Savannah came to an abrupt stop, her mouth dry and her heart pounding.

As if he were responding to her unspoken message, Rasch straightened up, leaned the shovel against the old barn they used as shelter for the elephants, and turned around. He'd known she was back from the moment she got out of the truck, but he'd waited for her to come to him. Now she had to speak first.

"Crusader, what in hell are you doing here?"

"I'm working."

"I can see that. Why?"

"It took me a while, but I finally figured it out, Gypsy. You held me responsible for the hurt you and your father suffered. Tifton is dead because of my decision to make an example of him. I can't change that even if I wanted to. But I can take his place. It won't be the same, but it's the best I can do."

"There's no way you can take Tifton's place."

"I know that." Rasch took a step forward. "I know what it is to blind yourself to a person's faults when you love that person. I'm sorry, Gypsy."

"No, don't touch me, Horatio Webber. Don't you lay a hand on me." Savannah folded her arms across her chest and held tight. She was shaking, fighting off an incredible urge to fling herself into his arms.

"I won't touch you, Gypsy. I know full well the danger in that. I've done a lot of thinking about us. We're too powerful together. We have only to touch and we're lost. This physical connection between us seems to close out everything else. I think it came too soon. We became lovers before we became friends. We're going to start over."

"Do you really think we could ever be merely friends, Crusader?"

"I don't know, but we're going to spend some

normal time together, get to know each other and find out."

"What about your job? A judge can't just join a circus, or do you plan to give up the bench."

"No, I can't turn my back on my responsibilities, but I can work here at night and on the weekends. I've already moved my things into a trailer that your father said wasn't being used. For now, I'm going to commute to Atlanta."

"I don't want you working here. I won't hire you."

"Too late, Gypsy, your father already has."

"But I want you—"

"I know," he interrupted, using a grin to break the tension, "but, like I said, I'm going to back off. You're going to have to stop lusting after my body and let me get back to work."

"Lusting after your body?"

"There's something basic about shoveling manure, don't you think?" he went on in a normal tone of voice. "Niko says it's good for my masculinity. It makes things grow."

Savannah gasped. The man was flirting with her. She could have said that if Judge Horatio Webber grew any more, his clothes wouldn't be able to conceal the parts of him she'd come to know so intimately, but she didn't.

"I thought you'd like that idea, darling." He smiled and turned back to his shovel.

"I don't know what you think you're doing, Crusader, but that isn't the kind of talk the public expects from a gubernatorial candidate. And I don't think this circus needs another clown."

"Oh, I'm not joking. This is a serious discussion about growth. Growth is change, and change is good for the soul. If I intend to be a good governor, I want to get back to basics, answer the needs of all the people. That's growth and change."

"Rasch, I don't think a lot of circus people vote. What makes you think the public will even consider a man who moonlights in the circus?"

"I think they'll like a man of the people. If not, I can always find a job with a shovel. There's a lot of manure in the world, Savannah, and I'm a man who doesn't back down from a mission. You ought to know that."

Rasch was here, in her circus, performing Tifton's chores. Savannah left immediately, taking Niko and a small troupe of performers to the orphanage, leaving Rasch and Alfred Ramey behind. While they were gone, Rasch and Alfred inventoried the circus, discarding equipment and costumes that were hopelessly worn out, and concentrating on refurbishing the remainder. Under Horatio's quiet guidance, Alfred began to oversee the operation of the circus for the first time since Tifton's death.

On her return, Savannah found herself without her usual job, so she began spending more and more of her time on the high wire, creating an aerial act with Niko, who had been in their original act before Tifton became the star and changed the focus of the act from flying to walking the wire. Tifton never wanted to catch; there was no glory there. By walking the wire, he could show his body to its best advantage.

Trying to work out a routine that was complex enough to entertain their audiences, Savannah began to combine her aerial act with their flying. Niko caught her when she flew through the air, and worked at her side as she walked the wire alone. She added flaming batons to her act, balancing on the wire as the fire twirled high over the spectators. The two functions merged, and a new act was born—not an especially spectacular one, but for now it was enough for the Flying Gypsies to be flying again.

The two-day engagement at the children's home had brought in enough money to repair the costumes and buy food for the troupe. Gradually word spread about the resurgence of the Ramey Circus, and former employees began to appear again, asking for their old jobs back.

Every day Judge Horatio Webber, dressed in a three-piece suit, left the grounds and reported to the courthouse. Once he left, Savannah's breathing returned to normal, and she took a long nap to compensate for the sleep she wasn't getting at night. Rasch made up for his lack of rest by napping at lunchtime and for an hour after court before he returned to the circus. Then, returning to his trailer, he stripped down to jeans and a sweatshirt and reported to Alfred Ramey for his next assignment.

The judge was pleasant and worked hard, speaking to Savannah, sharing little stories about his day, but nothing more. He joined her for meals in the cook tent and walked her to her trailer, then retired to his. While he didn't actually avoid Savannah, he made no attempt to be alone with her. She didn't know whether that was good or not. She only knew that she was very quietly going crazy.

New bookings were coming in for spring. Savannah scheduled the small-town fairs and shopping centers and passed on their good fortune to her father. But she could tell that his interest in the circus was waning. Alfred's heart wasn't in talking about where they'd go in the spring. More and more often she'd find Rasch overseeing the work, and Zeena and her father with their heads together, studying travel brochures and whispering about the past.

Rasch had been living on the grounds for two weeks, and their few conversations had been both brief and casual. Savannah watched him exercising the animals from her trailer. He still looked like a yuppie, but his hair was longer now, and the physical exercise had added a sleek, dangerous look to a body that continued to set Savannah on fire when she came into his vicinity.

She had to concede that Horatio Webber was good with the animals. He told them jokes, bad jokes, but Savannah heard and went around with her lips curved in a smile. He'd be good with children too. Savannah shook off that thought. Why on earth would she care about his rapport with children? He was learning to be a circus man. But his coloring didn't reflect the swarthy look of the Gypsies of old; he was more like the lusty blond animal trainers so popular in the big circuses. He didn't wear the glittery skintight costumes, and he carried a bucket instead of a whip, but she knew that the animals respected him. The members of the troupe respected him too. Even her father seemed to have forgotten that he'd once sworn to kill the man responsible for Tifton's death.

Savannah gave a little moan and pushed open her trailer door. She was wearing her practice clothes, a threadbare costume that had been retired from use. She poked her feet into the mules that protected her soft ballet slippers from the ground and strode to the tent. Every night she rehearsed alone until long after everyone else had retired for the evening. Only then could she work herself into a state of exhaustion to sleep.

Tonight the tension was worse than ever. She had a headache that intensified with every step she took toward the circus tent. Even when she was inside the tent, the tension didn't go away. She knew that Rasch was there, somewhere, watching. She left her mules on the sawdust-covered floor, found the bottom rung in the ladder, and began to climb.

"Gypsy? Could we talk for a minute before you begin?"

Savannah paused, the ladder swinging while she hesitated. Then it stopped. Rasch was there, holding it steady; he wasn't touching her, and yet she felt him as if they were pressed together like two magnets.

"What about?"

"Come down, Savannah. I like the view, but I can't talk while your tush is suspended in midair above me."

"Why don't you come up here with me?"

"I'm good with a shovel, Gypsy, but up there I'd be completely out of my element. I'm not sure that I could make any sense."

"Fine, then we'll match. Take off your shoes and join me. You want to live in my world, get to know the real me; here's where we begin."

Rasch groaned. Rationally he knew that there was a safety net beneath them; if he fell, he wouldn't be hurt. But emotionally he was already strung tighter than that high wire Savannah performed on, and he was afraid he'd snap.

She'd issued the challenge confident that he wouldn't accept.

She was wrong.

Rasch thought a moment. He had to do something to break through the wall of indifference she'd built around her. He smiled, unfastened his sneakers, and slid his jeans down his legs. He caught the swinging rope ladder in his hands, closed his eyes, and began to climb, quickly, before he lost his nerve. By the time Savannah reached the platform, Rasch was touching her feet with his hands. She pulled up, catching the bar to steady herself, and turned back to give Rasch a hand. He didn't need one. She couldn't hold back a gasp of surprise.

"Rasch, where are your clothes?"

"I left them down there."

"But you're practically naked! I mean, you're wearing only your underwear."

"I got your attention, didn't I?—just as you did when you appeared on my balcony."

"But that's unfair. How do you expect me to concentrate?"

Rasch let his gaze drift up her legs, pausing at the apex of her thighs and upward to her breasts. "I don't. Is this what you wore that night?"

"What do you want to talk about, Crusader?"

"Us. Jake thinks I'm moving too slow here."

"What does Jake have to do with this?"

Savannah reached back to get a better grip on the bar. Her movement made the platform sway, and Rasch grabbed for the bar, catching her between his hands. It was purely an instinctive reaction, she told herself. He wasn't making a move on her. He simply thought he was going to fall and reached out to steady himself. It wasn't his fault that she was between him and the bar he was clutching. She was in his arms, and he was instantly hard, pressing against the soft part of her stomach, his body overriding directions from his mind.

They connected, aware of what was happening but unable to stop the inevitable. "Oh, hell, Gypsy, I didn't mean to do this. I mean I don't—I won't—ah, hell!"

He hadn't meant to kiss her, but he couldn't stop his lips from taking what was offered.

She didn't mean to let him, but her arms were around his neck and she was holding him as if she were falling and he was her lifeline.

"Is this what you wanted, Crusader?" Her voice sounded as though it came from far away.

"No, I mean yes, this is what I wanted, but it isn't what I came for."

"It isn't?" Her mouth found his again, his kiss filling her with gentle joy. "Why did you come to the tent?"

"I wanted to invite you to a party."

"A party?" Her hands were around his body, tracing the strong muscles in his back.

"Yes, you know, a date. I spoke to your father. I think we've gotten past the getting-to-know-you stage. Your father gave me permission to—to—court you. Now I'm asking for a date."

"A date? To court me?" Savannah's head was swimming. One hundred feet in the air she was practically making love to the man who'd turned her life upside down. And now he was telling her that he had her father's permission to court her. "Why?"

"I've tried for weeks to show you that I could fit into your world. Now I want to show you that you can fit into mine. That's the right thing to do, Savannah. Jake convinced me that I owed it to us to bring you to his party."

She pulled away, trying to make sense out of what was happening. "Taking me to a party is Jake's idea? I think what Jake is trying to do is show you that I *won't* fit into your world."

"Are you going to let him?"

"I don't know. I'll have to think about it, and I can't think when we're touching. You know that."

"Fine, let's forget the thinking until later. The party isn't until this weekend. Right now the touching seems much more agreeable."

He'd grown bold, releasing the bar and planting his hands on her body for support. Little did he know that her legs had turned to cotton candy. Her arms rebelled against her will as she pulled him closer, claiming his lips again.

When Rasch finally pulled away, all his resolve to wait for her to come to him was gone. "Gypsy, Gypsy," he cajoled her, "come to my trailer. I want to touch your breasts, smell the tea olive blossoms, taste your skin. Please let me make love to you."

She jerked away, trying to sever the connection between them so that she could corral her frenzied emotions. "Make love to me in your trailer?" A cold shaft of air danced up her back. What was she doing? Every time he touched her, she melted. "No, stop it. You promised—" And then it happened.

Rasch lost his balance, and in trying to reach the

bar, fell against Savannah. She teetered wildly for a moment, then toppled backward from the platform.

"Savannah!" Rasch yelled, and reached for the rope ladder. It began to sway, and the scene below him blurred. He'd never get down to her on the ladder. After a quick, agonizing moment he moved to the opposite side of the platform, closed his eyes, and jumped.

His breathing stopped, and his body felt as if it turned inside out, but he survived, hitting the net and bouncing to a halt. He came to his knees and looked around. "Savannah, are you hurt?" He climbed across the swaying safety net to her side, losing his balance and falling across her.

"No, not unless you crush me with your rescue. That was a foolish thing to do, Crusader. You could have landed on top of me. I thought you fell."

"No, I jumped. I thought you were hurt."

Savannah wasn't hurt, but she felt the wall of ice crack. Climbing to the platform hadn't been easy, not even for Rasch, for jumping off must have been a nightmare for a novice. But he'd done it because he'd thought she was in danger. He'd come charging to her rescue again.

"Rasch . . . thank you. Are you all right?"

"I'm fine," he growled. He tried to stand, but the net seemed to be intent on swallowing him. The more he tried, the more of an idiot he felt. What made matters worse was the sound of Savannah's muffled giggle. Finally he was reduced to rolling toward the less malleable outside part of the net, catching the edge, pulling himself over, dropping to the sawdust beneath.

"So I'm not the most graceful thing in the world.

Stop enjoying my awkwardness. I could have been mortally wounded." He leaned against one of the support poles, pulled his jeans on, and jabbed his feet back into his sneakers.

Savannah stopped smiling. Maybe he was hurt. He'd never been trained in how to fall. She'd fallen, too, and she'd watched other members of her act fall, including Tifton, without it affecting her. But when she looked up and saw Rasch plunge off the platform, she'd felt her heart turn over.

"Where are you going? I need to examine you. I'm responsible for the safety of our employees. Let me look."

"No, Savannah, if you examine me, it will be for yourself, not because I'm your responsibility."

"I don't understand you, Crusader."

"I know. That's why we've been taking the time to know each other. That's why we're going to a party. And that's why I'm going back to work," he said, picking up his shovel.

"Why?"

"Because I promised your father that I would conduct a proper courtship. I don't think that making love to you in the sawdust is exactly what he was agreeing to."

"What makes you think I'd let you, Horatio Webber?"

"You would," he said seriously, his gray eyes turning to steel. "You will, but not yet." He took a step forward and winced. He must have hit his knee when he fell, Savannah thought.

She saw him frown and climbed down from the net.

"You *are* hurt."

"I hurt all right. I hurt every night. I hurt every time I see you. But it isn't my knee, and you can ease my pain, anytime you choose. We've both been so caught up in separating ourselves from a normal life that we don't know how to be lovers. I'm willing to wait for you, my Gypsy."

"But, Rasch—" *You don't have to wait,* she tried to say.

"Saturday night, Savannah. Wear something sharp. I'm going to take my girl to a party. We're going uptown."

"Are you sure you want me to be your girl?"

"I'm sure, Savannah Ramey. By the way," he added with that wicked grin she was beginning to recognize as the forerunner of some new sweet talk, "if you'd like to go to my apartment beforehand to dress, that can be arranged."

She gasped. "Your apartment? Why would I want to do that?"

"Because I have a shower, a nice hot shower, and I know how you'd like a shower."

"No thanks, I'll manage without one."

"Too bad, I'd like sharing your bath."

"Are you intentionally trying to drive me crazy?"

"I don't think so. How would it look for the governor's lady to be crazy?"

"Then make up your mind, Crusader. One minute you're pushing me away, and the next you're seducing me with your touch and your innuendos. Is that what you call a proper courtship?"

"I don't know. I've never conducted one before. I've never been—" He cut off his own sentence. *Never been in love before* was what he'd almost said. He stared at Savannah in disbelief. A relationship, yes.

Making Savannah care about him, yes. But love had never entered his mind, certainly not as a part of his plans for the future. He wasn't prepared for what he'd just learned. He'd never stopped long enough to consider loving a woman before. Now it made sense, explained why he was moonlighting in a circus. He'd thought it was a way to make up for Tifton's death.

He'd been wrong. Somewhere on that mountain trail he'd fallen in love with a Gypsy girl who'd showed him wildflowers and talked to animals. It had probably started to happen that first night on the balcony, and he hadn't realized it. But now the very thought of a lifetime of loving Savannah Ramey overwhelmed him.

Something of what he was feeling must have showed in his face, for Savannah reached out and touched his arm. "I'm sorry, Crusader, I've never known anybody outside of my circus family, and I guess I'm just afraid to take a chance. This is all new to me too."

She raised her eyes and took a deep breath. "All right, I'll go to the party with you if you're certain you want me too."

"I'm certain, Savannah." Holding her gaze, he leaned forward and brushed her lips. "Good night, Gypsy. If you run into any bears, my trailer door is always open."

Savannah stepped away, removing her fingertips from his shoulder. Lordy, what was she doing? Just over Rasch's shoulder she caught sight of the North Star gleaming brightly. *Yep, you've been caught, Savannah. You've eaten of the forbidden fruit.* Even when they weren't touching, she was held by the force of his presence. She turned around and ran.

Past the big tent, past the animal compound, she plunged between the trailers until she reached Zeena's quarters. Savannah knocked on the trailer door.

"Come in, Savannah."

Savannah pushed open the door and slipped inside, dropping into the chair beside Zeena's little kitchen table. "How did you know it was me? No, never mind. Just tell me—tell me what's happening. I don't understand."

"What don't you understand?" Zeena switched on a small lamp and sat down across from Savannah.

"This man—this judge who was responsible for Tifton's death—seems to think he can come here and take over our lives. He's charmed Father, you, all the hands, and now he thinks he's courting me."

"And that makes you unhappy?"

"It isn't that. I just feel so guilty. I mean, what about Tifton. What would *he* think?"

"If Tifton thought about it, which I doubt, he would probably figure out some way to work it to his advantage. Having a brother-in-law who was a governor would suit him just fine."

"You make Tifton sound like a ruthless opportunist."

Zeena sighed. "Ah, Savannah, Tifton was one of us and we protected him, but he was not what you thought he was."

"What I thought he was? He was my brother, and I loved him."

"Yes, and he used you and everyone he met. When are you going to see the truth? He *was* drinking. He *was* driving a stolen car, and he *did* almost kill that woman he hit. He was guilty, and for once he couldn't talk his way out of what he'd done. Have you ever considered what would have happened if the woman he hit had died?"

"But she didn't," Savannah protested irrationally, knowing that what Zeena said could have been true. "And besides, what about Father? He swore he would kill Horatio."

"Tifton was his only son. He lost Isabel, then Tifton—he was grieving, Savannah. He never would have gone through with any kind of revenge. Don't make him keep reliving his sorrow by burying yourself in blindness. Go with Rasch."

"You know that he invited me to a party Saturday night?"

"Yes. Are you going?"

"I don't know."

"You've never been afraid before, Savannah, why now?"

"Maybe," she admitted, "because it never mattered before.

Savannah let her hair dry in wild curls across her shoulders. She pulled on pale pink pantyhose spangled with stars, and applied a light frosting of silver eyeshadow to her lids and mascara to her long lashes. Dark rose-colored lipstick was followed by a whiff of her favorite cologne, and the trailer was filled with the smell of tea olive blossoms.

Glancing at her clock, Savannah began to hurry. Rasch would be at her door any minute, and her small trailer wasn't large enough for him to come inside. Her dress, rescued from her mother's trunk, was twenty-five years old, but the lines were ageless. Strapless pink satin stitched with sequins across the bodice and down the side of the fitted skirt, it was worn under a short pink jacket. Adding long glittery earrings that jingled like bells and a dusting of glitter in her hair, she leaned back and studied her reflection.

Perfect.

Tonight she looked like a royal princess. All she needed was a tiara and a coach. There was a knock. She picked up her bag and opened the door.

The coach she'd wished for was a black sports car. The man wearing the silly grin and holding out his hand was wearing a black tux. His hair had been cut, and lay perfectly on his head. He could have been an advertisement for some grand old hotel.

"Are you ready?"

As she took his hand, she knew that the connection had been made. She'd given him her answer, and there would be no turning back.

Eight

"So you're the one?"

Rasch and Savannah were greeted at the door by Jake Dalton, who took one look at Savannah and nodded.

"One what?" Savannah asked, eyeing Rasch's dark-haired friend curiously.

"The woman at the top of our party's hit list. I'm Jake Dalton, come in, I want to look you over."

Rasch tightened his grip on Savannah's elbow and glanced around. "Is it safe, Jake?"

Suddenly he was wary of entering the room. Maybe what he was doing was akin to throwing her to the lions, and he wasn't sure that the outcome, whatever it might be, was worth the chance he was taking.

Savannah leaned back and smiled up at Rasch. "Don't worry, Crusader, I'm tough, remember?"

"Yes, but these people in here are vultures. They don't respect their victims."

"Ah, but you forget, I can calm the savage beast."

Rasch stepped inside, sliding close to Savannah, and shut the door behind him, whispering in her ear, "The only savage beast you have to calm is me." He turned to Jake. "Why is Savannah on a hit list?"

Savannah turned to Jake. "Because I'm a possible liability, Crusader. Don't worry, Jake, I'm wearing my glass slippers. I disappear at midnight."

"Oh, no, you don't," Rasch contradicted her. "I have plans for after midnight, maybe even before. Do you have a balcony, Jake?"

Jake looked puzzled. "No, there's a patio, but since, as you well know, you're in a single-story house, a balcony would be a bit pretentious. Why?"

"I always like to check out all the exits. One never knows when there'll be a fire."

"Judge Webber," someone called from across the room. "I'd like to talk to you about your platform."

For the next hour Rasch smiled and charmed Jake's guests. Savannah was quickly accepted as Rasch's lady, and she found herself discussing the current "hot" issues when the only political dealings she'd ever had previously were about figuring out how to charm the local sheriff.

"What exactly do you do, Savannah?" a woman who'd been gazing at Rasch appraisingly asked during a lull in the political discussion.

"I'm—" she hesitated. Did she have the right to be honest at Horatio's expense? What would happen to his support if they discovered that she was a Gypsy whose father owned a circus? She settled for, "I'm a gymnast."

"Oh? Which events do you specialize in?"

"Savannah doesn't do that kind of gymnastics," Rasch said, coming to stand beside her and sliding his arm around her waist." She's a circus performer, an aerialist."

The woman gasped.

Jake groaned.

Savannah's eyes widened at the disclosure. She saw the surprise on the faces of the women gathered around her. She also saw what seemed to be pride in the gray eyes of the strong man whose arm was folded tightly around her waist. How could that be? Why would Rasch deliberately antagonize these people who were in a position to determine his future?

The crowd around them had grown quiet, then one man standing beside the window began to clap. "Bravo, Rasch, you picked a real woman. Do you walk the wires, or are you a flyer?" He started across the room toward them.

"Some of both." Savannah tried to make her voice firm, but it wavered in spite of her effort. "Our circus is very modest, so the cast of performers isn't large."

"Big isn't always better. My wife is an ice skater, a former Olympic champion. If she hadn't hurt her knee, she'd still be performing. Now she just gives lessons on a tiny little rink. But her pupils are future champions."

"Savannah," Jake introduced the newcomer with a broad smile, "this is Joker Vandergriff. He and his brothers own half the real estate in Atlanta, along with a sports medicine center and a few hundred other little businesses."

Rasch hugged the burly, red-bearded man. "Good to see you, old friend. What do you think of my lady?"

Joker took her hand, held it a long time, and gave her a warm, intimate smile. "She's got heart, Rasch, and she's strong. But what's most important is that she feels right."

Rasch nodded. "Joker is special, Savannah. According to his wife, he has healing power in his hands. She couldn't even walk when they met; now she's skating again."

Savannah understood what Rasch was saying. She could feel the balm in Joker Vandergriff's big hands. "Thank you, Joker. I'd like to meet your wife."

"Sure thing, we'll hold some kind of political shindig and raise a bunch of money for you, Rasch. Just name the date."

"Thanks, Joker. I knew I could count on you."

"There are still some questions to be answered, Judge Webber," the woman who'd asked Savannah about her profession said sharply. "I'm Lucille Peterson, and I'm a member of the party committee. It's important that a political candidate's *friends* be of high moral character. So far you don't have a breath of scandal associated with your career."

"You make me sound very dull, Lucille."

"Dull is safe, Horatio. Questionable behavior in a politician is out of style. I suggest you remember that if you expect to be governor."

Savannah felt the force of the campaign worker's gaze. She understood that the message was being leveled at her. *Don't mess with Judge Webber if you're a liability.* And a liability was just what she was. Nobody knew that better than she.

Rasch reclaimed his hold around Savannah's waist possessively, naturally. "Hear that, Joker? I might be questionable. Are you sure the Vandergriffs want to put their support behind me?"

"Absolutely," Joker's voice boomed out. "I've always been a gambler when I sense a sure thing. With my family's backing, your integrity, and a woman like this to come home to, you're bound to win."

After that, the tension vanished. Rasch and Savannah had passed the Vandergriff test, and every person in the room except Lucille Peterson, stopped by to speak to the candidate and his lady. Savannah had expected to be nervous. She wasn't—not about the party. It was what came after, with Rasch, that she didn't want to think about. And Lucille's words kept swimming around in her mind.

Relax, Savannah. You're just having a date, she told herself, nothing more. People don't sleep together on their first date.

No, the Gypsy part of her quipped, some people sleep together before they've even had a first date!

Not me, Savannah protested. I don't sleep around. I've never cared about a man before—not one I could hurt in so many ways.

And that was the problem. She cared.

Savannah caught sight of herself in a mirror above the buffet laid out with food and drinks. Her eyes were glowing. Her hair, a fine mass of ebony, sparkled with pink stars that caught and reflected the candlelight. The woman staring back was neither Savannah nor Gypsy. She was both.

At that moment she caught sight of Rasch behind her, watching her animated argument with herself. He simply slid his arms around her waist and nuzzled her behind her ear.

"Rasch, there are people watching."

"So there are. What do you say we find one of those exits and get out of here?"

"But isn't this party supposed to be for you?"

"No, this party was for you, Savannah. Jake wanted you to see that you could belong in my world as much as I belong in yours."

"You mean Jake wanted you to see that I didn't."

"Well, he was wrong, wasn't he? Can we go now?"

"I think you ought to shake a few more hands first. I haven't even tasted the food, and we haven't danced."

Before she could say anything else, he'd taken her hand and led her to the patio that Jake had referred to. There were several couples dancing to music being fed from a stereo concealed behind a bank of ferns.

Then she was in his arms, and everything and everybody faded away. "Actually, I don't think this is a good idea, Crusader."

"Why?"

"There are too many people watching."

"You're right." He took her hand and pulled her into the shadows. "Don't worry. It's all right for me to kiss you. I asked."

"Who did you ask?"

"Zeena. She said kissing was part of courtship and that it was perfectly acceptable."

"Perfect," Savannah cooed between kisses, between caresses. In her last moment of lucidity she added, "But I think you ought to know that I draw the line at lovemaking on a first date."

"Where is it?"

"What?"

"The line. I wouldn't want to step over it."

"Tell that to your—your body," she murmured.

"Too late, it isn't listening." He found the zipper in the back of her dress and slid it down, baring her breasts beneath his fingertips, spreading her body with liquid heat as he touched her.

"What are you doing, Crusader? Someone might come."

"Someone is damned well close to coming. Touch me, Gypsy. See what you do to me."

"I don't think that's a good idea, Rasch."

"Rasch—you called me Rasch! I love to hear you say my name, and I think that touching me is a very good idea." He pulled her hand down and pressed it against his body, the throbbing part of him that surged with heat at her touch.

"I know this isn't a good idea. Listen, Jake is calling us. I hear him. He's heading this way. Zip me up." She pulled away, tugging her dress over her breasts as she tried and failed to zip it closed.

"Damn Jake. Forget Jake. Let's get out of here." He glided farther into the shadows, pulling Savannah through the shoulder-high azaleas and past the magnolia tree.

"Rasch, the zipper's stuck!" What had been a wildly amusing interlude was suddenly a disaster in the making.

"Don't worry. I'll get us out."

There was a gate in the garden wall. Rasch slid the bolt, opened the door, and stepped through it, pulling Savannah behind him. Just as they exited into the driveway, a flash of light on the other side blinded them.

"Judge Webber, I'm Rob Henning, nightlife reporter for *Party Time*. Who is the lady?"

Rasch rushed past, shoving the reporter into the bushes, trying unsuccessfully to "accidentally" dislodge the camera. He managed to get Savannah to the car and start the engine before the reporter got untangled and followed.

"It doesn't matter, friend," the reporter yelled. "You don't want to talk to me, I'll find out who she is on my own. I have my sources."

"Oh, no, Rasch. He took my picture, with my dress falling off. You know what Lucille said; I've ruined your chances for political office."

"If my being governor is that shaky a proposition, then I won't be governor." Rasch stopped the car at the end of the drive, leaned across, and kissed her. His fingertips skimmed her neck and trailed across her breasts while his lips claimed hers again.

This time it was a car horn behind them that forced them apart. He pulled away, took a deep breath, and released the brake. "I'm sorry about your dress, Savannah, but I'll get you another one."

"Don't worry. At least I have a jacket. I think I can get back into my trailer without anyone knowing."

"Savannah, you can't get out of the car without someone knowing. That jacket doesn't button. It's much too skimpy, and there's nothing skimpy about your breasts."

She tried unsuccessfully to work on the zipper. She couldn't believe what had happened. What had she been thinking? She'd practically let him make love to her not fifty feet from a party of political contributors! No, that was wrong, it wasn't a matter of letting him. In another minute she would have unzipped his trousers, and they might both have been caught in a compromising position.

It wasn't Rasch she couldn't trust, it was herself. And it didn't matter who fit into whose world. When they were together, their world was each other, and nobody else mattered.

"Take me home, Rasch."

"I can't, Savannah. I'm tired of playing games. We need to be together, and we can't be together at the circus, not the way I want to. Come to the condo with me. Please?"

This time he didn't touch her. He kept both hands tightly on the wheel and waited for her to decide. It was her choice.

He was right. It was all she could do not to leap across the gearshift and fling herself into Rasch's lap. Going to his apartment meant making love. Was that what she wanted? Yes. Maybe not forever, but for tonight.

"All right, Rasch, I'll come."

He drove down Peachtree Street, north of Buckhead, and turned into a high-rise with lighted underground parking. They parked the car and took the elevator.

"This is certainly a much easier way to get to your apartment," Savannah said quietly.

The elevator stopped at the fourth floor. "How did you get out there that first night, on my balcony?"

"Niko rigged a wire between your apartment and a vacant one across the way. You didn't notice the wire in the darkness. I walked over and back."

He unlocked the door and turned on the light. "And the puff of smoke when you disappeared?"

"Circus tricks."

Rasch looked at Savannah. She stopped trying to hold up the dress top and let it fall.

"An illusion, planned to enslave me." He touched her hair. "I liked your hair blond, and red. But this is the way I like you best. Free and wild," he said in a hoarse voice, removing her short jacket in order to get to the zipper. He examined the offending piece of metal. It was caught by a tag of material. The more he worked at it, the tighter it caught.

His arm grazed her breast. Perspiration dripped down his face. He could no longer make his fingers cooperate. Finally, with an oath of exasperation, he gave both sides of the fabric a jerk, and the zipper broke. The dress, loosened from its restraint, slid down around her hips and fell in a pool of spangles around her silver high heels.

Rasch gasped and stepped back.

Savannah was wearing sheer, glittering pantyhose and nothing else. Her long, shapely legs would have made a Las Vegas dancer die of envy.

"Wild and free," he whispered. "And so very beautiful. God, how I want to make love to you, Gypsy."

"Then do it, Crusader, before we both incinerate!"

"Uh-oh, what about my promise to your father?"

"Did he ask you not to make love to me?"

"No, that was my idea."

"Some of your ideas are spectacular, Crusader. Some are not. This one isn't."

He nuzzled behind her ear, his hands touching and tormenting every secret place until she could no longer stand.

"Rasch, I'm dying. Love me, please."

"Always, my Gypsy, always." The pantyhose were gone, and so were Rasch's clothes. For the first time, they made love in a house, in a bed, in a blur of sensations that catapulted them with the intensity of a moon blast in a rocket ship into a shattering release.

Afterward, Rasch gathered her in his arms. "Savannah, maybe this isn't the time, but I want to tell you about Tifton."

"No. This is our time. I don't want to talk about him—not now." She twisted in his arms and pressed her face against his neck.

"Sometimes it's hard, making the best decision. I always tried to do the right thing, but I made everything black or white. By not allowing any gray, I could make my decision and put it behind me. If I could take it back, change my sentence, I would. I'm so damned sorry I made him my example."

"It's all right, Crusader. You never meant his death to happen."

But the moment had changed. And it was Rasch who was tense, not Savannah. Suddenly she understood how it must have been for Rasch, growing up without people around him to help cushion life's blows. As a child he'd had to grow up the best way he could, but underneath he wasn't sure. He had fear like everyone else, he just didn't show it.

"Rasch, it's all right. I understand. We've both been sailing along, set on a course that allowed little change of direction. We'd drawn very detailed maps. You'd right the world's wrongs, and I'd make my family's world right. Neither of us knew how to take any of the little side trips that make the trip worthwhile."

She felt him start to relax. His fingertips began to make tiny circles on the skin of her back, tiny warm circles that expanded as she talked.

"But Tifton wasn't just anybody, Gypsy. He was your brother, part of your plan."

"Yes, maybe he was. And it took him to bring us together."

"But—"

"Crusader. . . ." She lifted her face and cut off his protest with a kiss. "Crusader, maybe Tifton never had a map. He spent all his time on the side roads. A map is good just as long as it can be revised when the occasion warrants."

This time when Rasch kissed Savannah, it was such a sharing that she felt the last of his reserve melt away, and she learned that some side trips are very, very worthwhile.

After they made love again, they talked, not about serious things, but about cartoons, about the Beatles, and about libraries.

Rasch learned that under a special program a library would order and send books to people who couldn't come in.

Savannah learned that street gangs and peer pressure were as real as they were reported to be, that Rasch, too small to defend himself, had spent his childhood in the libraries she couldn't visit.

Correspondence courses offered the same opportunities to a circus performer that night school offered to a short-order cook determined to study law. One way or another, they'd both been thirsty for knowledge. From the beginning they'd traveled parallel paths that never should have intersected. And Savannah solved her last doubt by believing that only Gypsy magic could account for their being in each other's arms.

Long after midnight, in the middle of November under a harvest moon, they pulled the bedclothes out on the balcony and made love beneath the stars. Later Savannah slept in Rasch's arms, content and happy. Tonight was for loving, not regrets, and neither thought about tomorrow.

The next morning they made love again before Rasch left the apartment and made a quick trip to Lenox Square. There, he bought a plaid gathered skirt, a matching cotton sweater, and a pair of flat-heeled shoes.

"You didn't buy underwear," Savannah said as she unwrapped the packages.

"Sorry." He grinned. "An oversight."

"I'll bet."

"Only if you bet with me and the wager is agreeable," he said as he kissed her again.

"Rasch, if you don't stop kissing me, I'm going to have lips as big as mayonnaise-jar lids."

"Perfect match for some of my body parts, I'd say. Why don't you take those clothes off and come back to bed?"

"Judge Webber, is that the proper way to conduct a courtship?"

"Courtship! My gosh. Your father is going to have my hide. I'd better get you home."

"I don't think he has a shotgun, Rasch, but he has a whip. At least he used to," she teased.

"Good, a whipping I won't even notice."

The scars on his back. Savannah had noticed them before, that night at the campfire. Instantly she regretted her joke. "What happened, Rasch?"

"Oh, one of my mother's boyfriends was pretty quick with a belt."

"Your mother's boyfriend beat you?"

"Among other things."

Savannah was shocked. There were so many traumas in his past, so much that had kindled the determination he'd had to succeed. "Oh, Rasch, I'm so sorry. I can't imagine a mother allowing something like that to happen."

"Mothers do what they have to, I suppose. Mine did."

Savannah thought of her own mother and the pain she suffered. She remembered how hard Isabel worked to get better, and how the realization gradually came to her that she'd never be without pain anymore, that she'd never again fly through the air and land in her husband's arms.

"I guess mine did too. I was too young to understand how she could leave Tifton and me."

"Perhaps she left you because she couldn't bear to let you see her suffer. At least she knew what she was doing."

"Not at the end. There were so many drugs, she didn't know what she was doing. I'm sure she didn't know."

"Bad things kill even the innocent. And they kill a little part of those that live with the innocent too."

All the way back to the circus Savannah thought about what he'd said. Her mother had died from an overdose of drugs, and his mother had died from drugs too. Maybe her death was no accident either. She and Rasch had both lost a little part of themselves. Now maybe that little part was being replaced.

As they pulled into the parking lot, they were met by a crowd of cars and people.

"Judge Webber, what do you have to say about these charges?"

"Is she the one?"

"Ms. Ramey, how long have you been a member of a sex club? Who else belongs?"

Savannah and Rasch looked at the reporters and back at each other.

"What are you talking about?" Rasch asked a man he recognized from the press.

"Why, this." He held up a copy of *Party Time*. Covering practically the entire front of the tabloid was the picture of Savannah with her dress drooping across her breasts, her hair hanging in wisps around her face, and Rasch scowling angrily. They looked as if they'd been discovered in a compromising position and were hurrying to get away.

"Oh, no!" Savannah looked at the picture and the three-inch headlines. PROMINENT JUDGE CAUGHT IN SECRET SEX TRYST WITH GYPSY MADAM.

She didn't even want to read the article. What was said inside the paper didn't matter. The cover did enough damage. Judge Horatio Webber's career was ruined. He'd likely lose his seat on the bench, and the governorship was out of the question. And it was all her fault.

"Go inside, Savannah. I'll handle this." He opened the door and helped her out. The crowd of reporters swarmed around them, separating them in the confusion.

"What do you have to say, Ms. Ramey?"

She had to do something. These people weren't going to listen to reason. They were out for a story, and she was afraid that what they didn't learn, they'd make up—just like that awful man back at the wall. She couldn't let Rasch suffer on her account, not after he'd rescued her so many times.

At that moment she heard the mad cry of a crazed elephant as Nell thundered across the compound.

"Look out, there's an elephant."

"It's coming right over us."

"Move!" Niko charged Nell straight toward Savannah. Nell reached out and lifted Savannah with her big trunk, then trotted back the way she'd come.

"No, Niko. Stop her. I have to say something. Stop!"

Niko brought Nell to a halt. Savannah took Niko's hand and climbed up Nell's trunk to her big head, where she straddled the lovable old creature.

"May I have your attention, please," she said in a loud, clear voice.

The crowd hushed.

"I thank you for coming. The story you have is a lie. I'd like you to know the truth about the man who will be your next governor. Judge Webber cared enough to befriend the grieving sister of a man he had to pass sentence on. The judge is a fair and honest man who never did anything wrong. He's just a compassionate human being."

"You mean you aren't a madam?"

Savannah laughed easily. "I'm a member of the Flying Gypsies trapeze act. And I invite each of you to stop by my office and pick up some free tickets. Take pictures, talk to the workers if you like."

"How do you explain this article?"

"By telling you what happened. I was at a party, and my zipper broke. You all know Judge Webber's integrity. He was just trying to save me the embarrassment of having to face a house full of people." With an upraised hand she forestalled further questions.

"Perhaps you'd like to verify my story with the judge's campaign manager, Jake Dalton, before you spoil Judge Webber's chance at being the first real governor of the people."

An affirmative rumble began in the crowd. "Yeah. Super Judge is a good man."

"Maybe we'll check with Jake."

Savannah scanned the throng. She couldn't see Rasch. They'd been separated, and he'd been swallowed up by the crowd. Nell began to walk backward, moving away from the reporters, waving her trunk back and forth, warning them not to follow too closely. Finally, when they reached the elephant yard, Savannah slid down and fled into her trailer.

She'd known from the start that Rasch's world was a thousand miles from the circus, but she'd allowed her emotions to convince her that she and her crusader had a chance at a real relationship.

She ignored the first knock on the door. She ignored Rasch's plea that she let him in. She ignored her father's knock and closed out the pain she felt when he sent Rasch away.

Her plan to cast a love spell over the judge had worked too well. Never before had Savannah taken Zeena's words seriously. There was no such thing as

Gypsy magic; there couldn't be. But nothing else could explain what had happened. She'd become as enchanted as Rasch. Now she'd ruined his career, and her own life as well. Savannah fell across her bed, and for the first time since her mother's death, she cried herself to sleep.

"I'm sorry, Rasch," Alfred said, shaking his head, "she refuses to see you."

"But I love her. We have to talk."

"I know, but I told you in the beginning that you couldn't stay here if she didn't want you. And she doesn't—at least not now. You'll have to go."

Rasch stared at the old man with disbelief in his eyes. It couldn't end this way. Savannah had been an unplanned intrusion in his life, an intrusion that had given him such joy that he was willing to give up not only the governorship, but his position on the bench as well.

She understood him. She even forgave him for what he'd done. But more than that, they'd shared their loneliness and their dreams. They were right together, dammit, but she wouldn't let him come close anymore.

She thought that if she kept him away, he'd get his life back on track. That was why he loved her, because of her willingness to sacrifice herself for what she believed. He knew that Savannah cared for him. He'd held her, made love to her, shared in the incredible enchantment of their loving. She couldn't conceal, or erase, that. But she was sending him away.

Because she loved him.

And he had to go, because that was what she wanted and because he loved her too.

Rasch left Alfred's trailer and walked across the compound. He wandered over to the elephant area and petted Nell as she gave him wet kisses with her trunk. The cats were less responsive, but Rasch gained strength from their resigned acceptance of their fate. They didn't know the dangers of being free. Here they were safe and cared for. Here they had Savannah and the circus to protect them.

He took one long last look around.

"You know that she loves you."

Zeena stood at his side in a haze of moonlight, the crisp fall air tugging at her scarf.

"Yes, I know."

"And do you also know the circus is to be sold?"

"No. Why?"

"Because the family has ended. There is no one to carry on, at least no one for a long time."

He sighed. "And what should *I* do, Zeena? I don't know which way to turn."

"You go on with the course you have charted. If you are meant to be together, she will come to you in her own time, in her own way."

He turned away, stopped, and asked, "Zeena, tell me the truth, did you do it? Was it a Gypsy spell that brought us together?"

"You don't really believe that, do you?"

"I'm not sure. There was a time when I thought I had all the right answers. I was such a pompous fool. No, I guess I don't believe in superstition. I guess I just wanted to think that you might cast another spell. But she's gone. It's over, and I don't even have a glass slipper."

"You don't need a slipper, Crusader," Zeena said under her breath as she watched him go. A smile crossed her face, and she fingered the gold heart she wore on a chain around her neck.

"You have something better."

Nine

By spring all the circus animals had been sold. The trailers, booths of chance, and the food vendors were gone. Only the big top, patched and faded, remained.

Alfred and Zeena were making plans to take a trip to Europe. Savannah, who'd taken correspondence classes all her life, had enrolled in education classes at the local junior college and spent her free time working out with Niko on the wires.

Rasch had weathered the bad publicity generated by the *Party Time* article and was making good progress in his campaign for the governorship. He'd pulled ahead of his closest opponent for his party's nomination. But the fire had gone out of his eyes, and his decisions in the courtroom were more carefully rendered.

More tired than ever, Rasch found his duties in court weighed heavier and heavier. There were no more midnight visions, no more whiffs of the tea olive blossom, no more burning sensations on his body. The heat seemed to have gone out of his world. Through Niko he kept up with the circus, but Savannah still refused to see him. She had some misguided idea that she was protecting Rasch, and nothing would change her mind.

Rasch was worried. He drove out to Pretty Springs, the small town where the Vandergriffs lived. He needed to talk with Joker, the only other person who might understand the depth of his loss.

"I think I've got the nomination," Rasch explained. "But ever since Savannah sent me away, I've questioned every move I've made. If I don't figure out a way to get her out of my mind, I'm not even going to make a good dogcatcher, let alone do the kind of job I want to as governor. This is what I thought I wanted more than anything in the world, what I've worked for all my life. Now I don't seem to care."

"Let's examine the situation logically," Joker said. "If you do get Savannah back, your relationship might cost you the election. Do you think she could live with that?"

Rasch shrugged. "All I know is that she's too important for me to let her go. I was driven before I met Savannah. But I'd closed myself off from dreams, and beauty, and love. Sooner or later I'd have burned out, and I never even knew what I was doing."

Joker stood, pacing back and forth for a time before answering. "I think, my friend, that the problem will take care of itself, without our help. There is an aura around you, Rasch, when you and Savannah are together, an aura that dims with separation. I don't pretend to understand or explain it, any more than I can explain the healing powers of my hands.

But I say, give yourselves time. I think you'll find a way back to each other."

Rasch went back to Atlanta. Waiting was something he'd learned to do. But until now he'd never realized how difficult it would be.

Alfred and Zeena left for Europe.

Savannah completed one quarter in college and started another. If she couldn't perform for children, she'd find another way to reach them—as a teacher. She already had enough college credits, but she still needed the education courses required by the state.

Rasch was on her mind constantly.

She imagined him as a small boy, escaping to the library to study and learn, to avoid the bullies in his neighborhood, to resist the peer pressure on the street. The small traveling circuses were dying out; there were few circus children left, but there were still migrant workers, and the homeless, with no way to learn. Children reminiscent of Rasch and herself would be her charges. Rasch would be governor, and she would teach.

But she couldn't close off the memories, and she couldn't make new ones. She didn't eat well, and sleep came only after hours of physical exertion on the wire.

It was four o'clock on a Friday afternoon when Judge Webber gave up waiting and called a press conference at his office in the courthouse. His reception room was crowded with reporters who genuinely liked the popular man of the people. They approved of his openness and honesty and supported his plans to be governor. When he entered the room, the noise quieted instantly.

Camera lights lit up.

Tape recorders were switched on.

Pencils were poised in readiness to be used.

"Ladies and gentlemen of the press, I've called you here to make an announcement. As you know, I have been actively campaigning for the governorship of the state of Georgia on a platform of honesty and reform. But I am considering withdrawing myself as a candidate, and I want to let you know why."

After a roar of surprise and shouted questions, Rasch lifted his hand and asked for silence. "I'm certain that you remember the incident with *Party Time* where Ms. Savannah Ramey and I were accused of being sexually involved."

"Yes!"

"We remember, are you suing?"

"No, I'm *wooing*. I want to marry Savannah Ramey, and I want you to be the first to know that I intend to do everything in my power to convince her to become my wife."

"A circus performer as our first lady?" A reporter asked incredulously.

Rasch's gaze found the reporter and silenced him with its intensity. "Why not? If I'm elected, you'll have the son of a drug addict for a governor. I am what I am, and my background is what it is. I can't change that. I wouldn't want to. I wouldn't want to change Savannah either."

"But doesn't she have a questionable background?"

"That's what I want you to know. Her brother, Tifton Ramey, was arrested on a DUI accident charge.

He was tried and found guilty. I sentenced him to jail, where he got into a fight with another inmate and was killed."

"That Ramey kid. Yeah, we remember," one of the reporters said.

"Savannah's mother died when she was a child. There is only her father left. The Ramey Circus, over my objections, has been sold, but if it hadn't, and if Savannah wanted to continue to perform, I would be pleased to have her do so."

This time there was a stunned silence in the room. Then, from the back corner, a journalist began to clap. Soon she was joined by a host of others. And as the clapping intensified, Rasch felt the vest of ice he'd worn around his heart for weeks begin to melt.

His pulse quickened. There was no guarantee that the public would agree, but the press seemed to understand and support his position. He felt a lightness sweep over him, and an ever so intense longing.

Savannah, he wanted Savannah, and he was going to her. He'd let himself be pushed away, let her protect him with her rejection, let her disappear from his life when he needed her beside him.

Success and prestige had been his goal, what he'd worked for all his life, but without someone to share it with, success was empty. Both his mother and Savannah's mother had found their personal lives too painful to continue, but they'd left a legacy behind, their children.

He and Savannah belonged together. Rasch nodded to the reporters, expressed his thanks for their support, and backed into his office and out the back corridor to escape from their questions.

A clatter in the hallway behind him told him that

the media people had guessed his intentions and were following. He cut through an occupied courtroom and took the exit stairs to the basement.

Sliding behind the wheel of his truck, he drove away, singing loudly:

"Oh, Savannah, don't you cry for me. I'm headed for the circus with my heart a-flying free." And that's what he was doing, just as fast as the speed limit would allow.

From the highway he could see the smoke. From the dirt road across the field he could see the flames. One corner of the big top was on fire.

Savannah! Her flaming batons.

He parked the car and broke into a run. The entire corner of the tent was engulfed. "Savannah! Niko!"

The flap of the tent was open, just as it was when Savannah was rehearsing. Clouds of smoke billowed from inside. Curls of flames danced across the sawdust. He could barely see. Ripping off his coat and tie, Rasch covered his face with his jacket and ran inside. Where was she? On the high wire. He began to climb the ladder.

He didn't feel the beam when it toppled over. He never knew what hit him when he fell. There was only the heat of the fire, and his fear. "Savannah!"

Inside her trailer Savannah came suddenly awake. "Rasch!" Something was wrong. She felt the paralyzing fear of separation as if half of her had been cut away. He was hurt. He needed her. She sprang to her feet and looked out the window. Then she saw it—the fire, Rasch's truck, and his tie on the ground between.

"Niko!" But Niko had gone into town. There was no one but her, and the man she loved was inside.

Savannah wet a towel, flung it over her shoulders, slid her feet into her shoes, and raced across the compound and into the tent. "Rasch, where are you?"

Everything seemed to be burning, even the sawdust curls on the floor. She could see nothing but smoke. Her eyes began to water, and she could hardly breathe. Then she saw him, in the net. One end of it had been hit by a falling support beam. The net and the beam were hanging at a crazy angle, slanting downhill to the floor. And beside the beam was Rasch. He wasn't moving.

Little flames were licking the curls of sawdust below, and the supposedly fireproof tent was in flames everyplace it had been patched. Savannah looked for a way to reach the man she loved.

"Rasch!"

Savannah couldn't get across the floor, but she leapt for the metal ladder. It didn't quite reach the floor, and the portion of the tent over the ladder and platform was still intact. She began to climb. The air at the top was unbreatheable. Savannah covered her mouth and nose with the wet towel, took a deep, smoky breath, and held it. At the top she loosened one of the ropes once used by Tifton when he did his rope-spinning act. With a prayer that the rope was still intact, she lowered herself to the net.

"Rasch!" She let out the air she'd been holding and took in another breath, choking and gagging. "Please, you have to help me!" She made her way to his side and looped the rope beneath his arms, around his upper body. At that moment the frame for the net began to creak. The extra weight on one end was pulling the other side in. They were four feet off the ground. Maybe—

Savannah put her arms around Rasch and held on tight. The frame collapsed, but they were swinging in the air. Savannah began to use the motion of her body to increase the distance of their swinging. The fire beneath their feet was beginning to die down. Thank goodness for poverty. If they'd been able to afford fresh shavings, both she and Rasch would have roasted toes by now.

She alternated the wet towel between them. But it was drying rapidly in the heat. Her feet finally hit one of the surviving support poles. She gave a big push. If they didn't suffocate; if she could get the rope to swing out far enough. If the rope didn't burn. If Niko would come.

Too late. The rope broke, dropping them to the smoldering floor just inside the doorway, away from the worst of the glowing coals but still inside the burning sawdust.

Quickly Savannah came to her feet. "Rasch! Rasch, please, you've got to get up." Her pleas urged the groaning man to his feet. After a few anxious moments he stumbled after her.

Around the tent and onto the edge of the woods they struggled until Rasch collapsed. He didn't appear to be burned anywhere. But he was very still. She wiped away the soot on his face and found an egg-size lump over his right eye. Laying her head against his chest, she heard his heart beating, though his breathing was shallow and uneven.

"Don't die, Rasch. I won't let you! I need you!"

There was a time when she'd set out to kill him, to

take revenge for her brother's death—before she'd begun to understand the man, to know how important he was in her life. Since she was a child, she'd closed off her own needs in order to take her mother's place. She didn't need to do that anymore.

All she needed for her entire life was in her arms, her crusader who'd charged to her rescue again.

At least Rasch was still breathing. It was the lump on his head that she was worried about, and the cold, clammy feel of his skin in all the heat.

"Oh, Rasch, you crazy, wonderful fool. You've gone and hurt yourself on my account—bad."

"Gyp . . . Gypsy . . . love you."

She heard his gravelly whisper. At least she thought she did, but he lapsed into unconsciousness again, and this time she thought he had died.

Climbing to her feet, Savannah raced back to her trailer. She had no phone and no transportation. She couldn't call for help. "Oh, Niko, please hurry."

Gathering up blankets and wet towels, she started back across the compound. Just as she reached the woods, she heard the sirens. In amazement she watched as a fire truck, two police cars, and an ambulance raced across the field. Savannah began to wave her arms. The rescue van screeched to a halt, and the paramedics piled out.

In less than five minutes the fire was under control. Rasch had been loaded into the wagon, and they were racing down the highway to the hospital. The paramedics recognized the man they expected to be the next governor, and worked feverishly on him all the way.

The emergency room was waiting for them, personnel standing by to take Rasch in to the waiting doctors, who set events in motion. Savannah collapsed in the waiting room, covered with soot and paralyzed with fear. The admissions clerk came over and sat down beside her, clipboard in hand.

"Could you answer some questions, Ms. Ramey?"

"Ms. Ramey? You know who I am?" Savannah was confused. Had Rasch regained consciousness?

"After the judge's press conference today, everybody in the state knows who you are."

"What press conference?" The woman was talking about press conferences when Rasch might be dying.

"Honey, he told the world today that he was going to marry you. If that meant he wouldn't be governor, he'd do something else. If they don't want him to be a judge anymore, that's fine too. I think it's wonderful, offering to give up everything for love."

"Rasch stop being a judge? No, I won't allow it." She charged to her feet and paced angrily back and forth. "How dare he even consider such a thing! He's fair, and kind, and he's honest. What else would you want in a judge?"

"Not a thing, honey. Nobody's going to let them throw him out of office. The people elected Horatio Webber as judge, and the people are going to elect him governor. And you're going to be the governor's lady."

The doctor finally decided that except for a mild concussion and some sore ribs, Rasch would be as good as new after a full night's rest. He was half asleep when Savannah opened the door to his hospital room. He didn't have to open his eyes; he recognized her exquisite smell.

"Tea olive blossoms. Gypsy? Gypsy, you're all right?"

His kind gray eyes struggled to open as Savannah leaned over him.

"Of course I'm all right, you insane, beautiful man. What did you think you were doing?"

"Saving you. I thought you were inside, with your batons. The tent was on fire."

"And you climbed up the ladder to rescue me."

"Of course. We're going to get married, you know."

"I know. The entire world knows, Horatio Webber. You held a press conference, remember? It's on the front page of the evening paper, and on every newscast from here to the state line."

Rasch smiled. "Well, I thought it would be easier that way. Have I told you that I love you?"

"I think you did."

"Did I ask you to marry me?"

"No, I think you just told me that I was going to."

"Did you say yes?"

"I haven't yet."

"But you will. We belong together, Savannah. I think we ought to get married right away. Send for a judge."

"You're a judge, darling, couldn't you marry us?"

"Not legally, but if you'll crawl into this hospital bed with me, I'll perform a temporary ceremony, just till we can do it right." He unsuccessfully fought back a yawn, and felt his eyes closing in spite of his attempts to stay awake.

But they were connected. Savannah was there, holding his hand, and even in sleep he felt her presence.

Savannah considered his request. She might have

joined him, but he needed his rest. Besides, she didn't need anybody's approval. Rasch wanted her, and she wanted him.

That was all either of them needed, even without a Gypsy spell. They'd known that from the beginning, hadn't they?

The chrome clock chimed the hour: midnight. A wall of blooming tea olive trees planted in big tubs edged the patio, saturated the air with their sweet fragrance. There were tiers of candles casting crazy shadows on the floor and sending little puffs of smoke into the June night air.

Savannah stood on the patio in a blaze of moon-light, gazing into the eyes of the man she was about to marry. Her black hair was as fine as gossamer silk, woven with lace and silver ribbons. Her wedding dress, made of chiffon, draped her body like a hundred shimmering veils, sprinkled with moondust and stars. She carried a bouquet of pink roses interspersed with dark green leaves and the tiny clusters of blossoms from the tea olive trees behind them.

Rasch stood proudly beside her in his white suit. There was one sweetheart rosebud and a green stem filled with tiny tea olive blossoms tucked into his lapel. She allowed her eyes to feast on the picture of this beautiful man whose hair had grown long again, curling along the top of his collar, its pale color catching the light of the moon and turning into spun gold in its illumination.

Free and wild.

The past touched the present.

Silver melded to gold.

The judge and the Gypsy joined their lives forever in a ceremony they wrote themselves. They promised honesty and commitment, love and devotion, and a lifetime of enchantment to each other.

Afterward, Niko, Jake Dalton, the Vandergriffs, a few judges, and Rasch's election committee joined the members of the press in toasting the bride and groom. There was a wedding cake with fig icing and punch flavored with pomegranates. "Fit for the gods," Rasch insisted before making a second toast to the absent Alfred Ramey and Zeena, who had telegrammed their best wishes from Hungary.

The next night, beside Shadow Lake, beneath a sky filled with glittering stars, Savannah and Rasch pledged their love in the light of a Gypsy moon. Savannah donned her red print skirt and peasant blouse and shyly danced for her chosen mate around the open campfire, speaking the words of the heart with her body as she made her pledge of eternal love.

The only music was the sound of her ankle bells, the wind in the trees, the water lapping at the shore, and the castanets she carried in her hands. With time-treasured moves she wove her spell of love and desire, until at last Rasch reached out and caught her hand, bringing her into his arms, against his heart.

"My Gypsy woman," he whispered as he covered her mouth with his lips. "Mine. It was here, that first night, that I fell in love with you. I wanted you then, but never more than now."

Rasch removed their clothes, checking his impatience to feel her bare skin against him. Threading his fingers through the strands of hair across her shoulders and down her back, he took her lips gently, his tongue moving lightly inside her mouth.

Savannah moaned as Rasch pulled away and nibbled along her jaw and down her neck. Every touch was a slow, seductive movement, as if he were choreographing it to music—touching, building, then pulling back. She shivered deliciously as he caught her nipple inside his hot wet mouth, then released it over and over again, then moved down her body in lazy, delicious exploration.

As he touched her, it was as if he'd joined her dance. Slowly, sensually, with his body and his heart he loved her. And every part of her was responding; a tingling weakness changed into a jolt of sensation as he slipped his hand between her legs and parted her, dipping into the trembling valley now arching to meet his touch. His other hand found her breasts and brushed her nipples gently with his fingertips while the lower hand slid away to allow his lips to caress the core of her desire.

"Rasch . . ."

"What, sweetheart?"

But she didn't answer. Instead, Rasch heard a low, sweet moan as she began to tremble. He was only now beginning to understand what it meant to give pleasure, to find joy in giving joy.

"Oh, Rasch," she said hoarsely as his lips began to move back up her body, leaving her hot and aching. "What kind of magic have we found?"

"It isn't magic, Gypsy, it's love. Everlasting love." Rasch moved over her. Tell me that you love me, Savannah Webber, as much as I love you."

"Oh, yes."

As if in a dream, they joined and soared to the

heavens, surrounded by midnight sky and stars so close that they could reach out and touch them. There was a heat that grew ever more intense, releasing into a shuddering arc of pleasure that showered the night with fire. Then, in a dreamlike state of fantasy, they fell back down, down, down, to earth and reality.

The lake took form once more. They were lying on the open sleeping bag, naked bodies entwined, sated with the rhapsody of their love.

How much he loved this woman, how right they felt together.

"Oh, Rasch, look!"

Two shooting stars fell dramatically across the heavens, followed almost immediately by a virtual shower of iridescent light.

"A rocket," Rasch said, "releasing a barium cloud."

"Oh, no," Savannah corrected him. "It's the North Star. She's been freed to follow her heart. Don't you see? All the heavens are celebrating."

"Of course. They're watching us." Then, growing serious, he said softly, "You won't regret closing the circus?"

"Perhaps," she admitted, folding her arm across his chest. "But the loss of one part of life opens a door for the next part to begin. You're going to be the best governor the state has ever had. And I'm going to teach children who need to learn to dream." She sighed. "Oh, Rasch, you've made me feel so cherished. I never knew that love could be like this. The only regret I have is that Father and Zeena aren't here."

"On our honeymoon?" Rasch gasped.

"Of course not! You know what I mean. I want them to know how happy we are."

Rasch smiled. "My darling Gypsy, I have the feeling that they already know."

Then Savannah was sliding over him, tasting, examining him with her tongue. Her dusky-rose nipples skimmed his chest. "You're right. You know, Crusader, you called me Gypsy, but it was you who cast the spell, a spell of place and belonging." She smiled and claimed his lips for a moment, released them and moved on to skim his eyebrows with her lips.

"A spell of place and belonging," he repeated, and felt a great wave of understanding sweep over him. That's what he'd been seeking too. He'd tried to make it happen with a system of laws and justice, but it had taken a Gypsy woman to teach him that real belonging was a place in the heart.

"We'll name our first child Atlanta, for the city in which she's born," Savannah mused. "I hope you don't mind continuing the Ramey tradition?"

"Tradition. I think I like that."

"Good." She slid lower, catching the male part of him in the lovely crease between her legs. "Then it's all right with you that our first child will be a girl?"

"A girl?" Rasch knew he was smiling. "That's wonderful! How do you know?"

"I know," she said quietly as she lifted herself over him. He tried to remain still as she lowered her body, slowly, maddeningly, imprisoning him inside her body.

Rasch didn't doubt her knowledge. "What about the second? I haven't said anything, but— Washington might be nice."

Her lips moved across his forehead and down his neck. She could feel his body begin the motions of love beneath her.

"Washington? Senator Webber? I quite agree. After that," she whispered, tightening her muscles about the deep, pulsating heat that moved insistently against her, "who knows? Jupiter, or maybe Orion. Ah, my darling Crusader, the galaxy has no limits for the judge and his Gypsy."

THE EDITOR'S CORNER

As winter's chilly blasts bring a rosy hue to your cheeks and remind you of the approaching holiday season, why not curl up in a cozy blanket with LOVESWEPT's own gift bag of six heartwarming romances.

The ever-popular Helen Mittermeyer leads the list with **KRYSTAL,** LOVESWEPT #516. Krystal Wynter came to Seattle to start over in a town where no one could link her with the scandalous headlines that had shattered her life. But tall, dark, and persistent Cullen Dempsey invades her privacy, claiming her with an intoxicating abandon that awakens old fears and ensnaring her in a web of desire that keeps her from running away. A moving, sensual romance—and another winner from Helen Mittermeyer!

LOVESWEPT's reputation for innovation continues as Terry Lawrence takes you right up to the stars with **EVER SINCE ADAM,** #517, set in an orbiting station in outer space! Maggie Mullins is there to observe maverick astronaut Adam Strade in the environment she helped design—not to succumb to his delicious flirting. And while Adam sweeps her off her feet in zero gravity, he fights letting her get close enough to discover his hidden pain. Don't miss this unique love story. Bravo, Terry, for a romance that's out of this world!

Please give a rousing welcome to Patricia Potter and her first LOVESWEPT, **THE GREATEST GIFT,** #518. Patricia has already garnered popular and critical success with her numerous historical romances, and in **THE GREAT-EST GIFT** she proves her flair with short, contemporary romance, as well. Writing about a small-town teacher isn't reporter Lane Drury's idea of a dream assignment—until she meets David Farrar. This charming rogue soon convinces her she's captured the most exciting job of all in a romance that will surely be a "keeper." Look for more wonderful stories from Patricia Potter in the year to come.

Let Joan J. Domning engulf you with a wave of passion in **STORMY'S MAN,** LOVESWEPT #519. Gayle Stromm certainly feels as if she's in over her head with Cass Starbaugh, who's six feet six inches of hard muscles, bronzed skin, and sun-streaked hair. Gayle's on vacation to escape nightmares, but caring for the injured mountain climber only makes her dream of a love she thinks she can never have. Cass can't turn down a challenge, though, and he'd do anything to prove to Stormy that she's all the woman he wants. An utterly spellbinding romance by the incomparable Joan J. Domning.

Marvelously talented Maris Soule joins our fold with the stirring **JARED'S LADY,** LOVESWEPT #520. Maris already has several romances to her credit, and you'll soon see why we're absolutely thrilled to have her. Jared North can't believe that petite Laurie Crawford is the ace tracker the police sent to find his missing niece, and, to Laurie's dismay, he insists on joining the search. She's had enough of overprotective men to last a lifetime, yet raw hunger sparks inside her at his touch. Together these two create an elemental force that will leave you breathless and looking for the next LOVESWEPT by Maris Soule.

IRRESISTIBLE, LOVESWEPT #521 by beloved author Joan Elliot Pickart, is the perfect description for Pierce Anderson. This drop-dead-gorgeous architect thinks he's hallucinating when a woman-sized chicken begs him to unzip her. But when a dream girl emerges from the feathers, he knows the fever he feels has nothing to do with the flu! Calico Smith struggles to resist the sensual power of Pierce's kissable lips. She's worked so hard for everything she has, while he's never fought for what he wanted—until now. Another fabulous romance from Joan Elliott Pickart.

And (as if these six books aren't enough) LOVESWEPT is celebrating the joyous ritual of weddings with a contest for you, a contest that will have three winners! Look for details in the January 1992 LOVESWEPTS.

Don't forget FANFARE, where you can expect three superb books this month. **THE FLAMES OF VENGEANCE** is the second book in bestselling Beverly Byrne's powerful trilogy. From rebellion plotted beneath cold, starry skies to the dark magic that stalks the sultry Caribbean night, Lila Curran's web, baited with lust and passion, is carefully being spun. Award-winning Francine Rivers delivers a compelling historical romance in **REDEEMING LOVE**. Sold into sin as a child, beautiful, tormented "Angel" never believed in love until the strong and tender Michael Hosea walked into her life. Can their radiant happiness conquer the darkest demons from her past? Much-acclaimed Sandra Brown will find a place in your heart—if she hasn't already—with **22 INDIGO PLACE**. Rebel millionaire James Paden has a dream—to claim 22 Indigo Place and its alluring owner, Laura Nolan, the rich man's daughter for whom he'd never been good enough. Three terrific books from FANFARE, where you'll find only the best in women's fiction.

As always at this season, we send you the same wishes. May your New Year be filled with all the best things in life—the company of good friends and family, peace and prosperity, and, of course, love.

Warm wishes from all of us at LOVESWEPT and FANFARE,

Nita Taublib

Nita Taublib
Associate Publisher, LOVESWEPT
Publishing Associate, FANFARE

FANFARE

On Sale in December

CARNAL INNOCENCE

☐ (29597-7) $5.50/6.50 in Canada
by Nora Roberts
bestselling author of GENUINE LIES

*Strangers don't stay strangers for long in Innocence, Mississippi, and secrets have
no place to hide in the heat of a steamy summer night. A seductive new novel from
the master of romantic suspense.*

A ROSE WITHOUT THORNS

☐ (28917-9) $4.99/5.99 in Canada
by Lucy Kidd

*Sent from the security of her Virginia home by her bankrupt father, young
Susannah Bry bemoans her life with relatives in 18th century England until she
falls in love with the dashing actor Nicholas Carrick.*

DESERT HEAT

☐ (28930-6) $4.99/5.99 in Canada
by Alexandra Thorne

*Under an endless sky, lit by stars, three women ripe with yearning will dare to seize
their dreams -- but will they be strong enough to keep from getting burned
by . . . Desert Heat?*

LADY GALLANT

☐ (29430-X) $4.50/5.50 in Canada
by Suzanne Robinson

*A daring spy in Queen Mary's court, Eleanora Becket would risk all to rescue the
innocent from evil, until she herself is swept out of harm's way by Christian de
Rivers, the glorious rogue who ruled her heart.*

FANFARE

Rosanne Bittner
_____ 28599-8 EMBERS OF THE HEART . $4.50/5.50 in Canada
_____ 29033-9 IN THE SHADOW OF THE MOUNTAINS
$5.50/6.99 in Canada
_____ 28319-7 MONTANA WOMAN .... $4.50/5.50 in Canada

Dianne Edouard and Sandra Ware
_____ 28929-2 MORTAL SINS .... $4.99/5.99 in Canada

Tami Hoag
_____ 29053-3 MAGIC .... $3.99/4.99 in Canada

Kay Hooper
_____ 29256-0 THE MATCHMAKER, ... $4.50/5.50 in Canada
_____ 28953-5 STAR-CROSSED LOVERS .. $4.50/5.50 in Canada

Virginia Lynn
_____ 29257-9 CUTTER'S WOMAN, ... $4.50/4.50 in Canada
_____ 28622-6 RIVER'S DREAM, ... $3.95/4.95 in Canada

Beverly Byrne
_____ 28815-6 A LASTING FIRE .... $4.99/ 5.99 in Canada
_____ 28468-1 THE MORGAN WOMEN .. $4.95/ 5.95 in Canada

Patricia Potter
_____ 29069-X RAINBOW .... $4.99/ 5.99 in Canada

Deborah Smith
_____ 28759-1 THE BELOVED WOMAN .. $4.50/ 5.50 in Canada
_____ 29092-4 FOLLOW THE SUN .... $4.99/ 5.99 in Canada
_____ 29107-6 MIRACLE .... $4.50/ 5.50 in Canada

Ask for these titles at your bookstore or use this page to order.
Please send me the books I have checked above. I am enclosing $ _____ (please add
$2.50 to cover postage and handling). Send check or money order, no cash or C. O. D.'s
please.
Mr./ Ms. _____
Address _____
City/ State/ Zip _____
Send order to: Bantam Books, Dept. FN, 414 East Golf Road, Des Plaines, IL 60016
Please allow four to six weeks for delivery.
Prices and availablity subject to change without notice.   FN 17 - 12/91

THE LATEST IN BOOKS
AND AUDIO CASSETTES

Paperbacks

☐	28671	**NOBODY'S FAULT** Nancy Holmes	$5.95
☐	28412	**A SEASON OF SWANS** Celeste De Blasis	$5.95
☐	28354	**SEDUCTION** Amanda Quick	$4.50
☐	28594	**SURRENDER** Amanda Quick	$4.50
☐	28435	**WORLD OF DIFFERENCE** Leonia Blair	$5.95
☐	28416	**RIGHTFULLY MINE** Doris Mortman	$5.95
☐	27032	**FIRST BORN** Doris Mortman	$4.95
☐	27283	**BRAZEN VIRTUE** Nora Roberts	$4.50
☐	27891	**PEOPLE LIKE US** Dominick Dunne	$4.95
☐	27260	**WILD SWAN** Celeste De Blasis	$5.95
☐	25692	**SWAN'S CHANCE** Celeste De Blasis	$5.95
☐	27790	**A WOMAN OF SUBSTANCE** Barbara Taylor Bradford	$5.95

Audio

☐	**SEPTEMBER** by Rosamunde Pilcher Performance by Lynn Redgrave 180 Mins. Double Cassette	45241-X	$15.95
☐	**THE SHELL SEEKERS** by Rosamunde Pilcher Performance by Lynn Redgrave 180 Mins. Double Cassette	48183-9	$14.95
☐	**COLD SASSY TREE** by Olive Ann Burns Performance by Richard Thomas 180 Mins. Double Cassette	45166-9	$14.95
☐	**NOBODY'S FAULT** by Nancy Holmes Performance by Geraldine James 180 Mins. Double Cassette	45250-9	$14.95

Bantam Books, Dept. FBS, 414 East Golf Road, Des Plaines, IL 60016

Please send me the items I have checked above. I am enclosing $_____
(please add $2.50 to cover postage and handling). Send check or money order,
no cash or C.O.D.s please. (Tape offer good in USA only.)

Mr/Ms _____

Address _____

City/State _____ Zip _____

FBS–1/91

Please allow four to six weeks for delivery.
Prices and availability subject to change without notice.